Twisted Fairy Tales for Adults

An Anthology

Erisa Apantaku
Emily Brooks
Laurel Bucholz
C.K. Hugo Chung
Hugo Glin
L.L. Phelps
Nick Vaky
Pat Woods
Whitney Zahar

Cover by James
humblenations@gmail.com

Also by Taipei Writers Group

Taiwan Tales

Night Market: An Anthology

Peak Heat: An Anthology

Praise for *Taiwan Tales*

"A diverse collection of enjoyable, well-written short stories ... an excellent window into the expatriate experience of Taiwan ... also a native reflection on Taiwanese culture."
Centered on Taipei

"... more than a brief touristy description of the island nation, but rather a perceptive look into the small country through the eyes of foreigners who have all at one point in their lives called Taiwan their home."
China Post

"There isn't a weak link anywhere in it ... most definitely recommended reading ... in every way an outstanding compilation."
Taipei Times

For more information about our previous anthologies and all forthcoming projects by the Taipei Writer's Group, sign up to the TWG Anthologies Club.

http://eepurl.com/bg3dHn

We will not send SPAM or pass on your details

The Twisted Tales

Cynder and the Magical Bucket
Fed up with 'happily ever after,' Cynder successfully moves on with her life, only to meet a bunch of damsels in distress needing to do the same. This story contains plenty of foul language, and a lot of laughs to accompany it.

The One Who Bleeds
According to legend, a king riding on a horse that sweats blood will conquer the world. One king has found such a horse, but can he force the animal to yield to him?

Heart/Clock
Beth is stressed. Beth's heart is stressed. One morning, Beth wakes up and sees her heart beating on her bedside table.

Justify My Love
A kid disappears. Facing a relentless investigation, the Snake sisters must decide how far they will go to protect their family.

Whispers
After receiving devastating injuries from a makeshift bomb, a female soldier meets a seductive *jinn* and gets three wishes.

Li Man and the Fox Spirit
When the poet Li Man encounters a beautiful fox spirit, events do not turn out exactly how either of them had planned.

Matchstick Fallout
Tiffany, a recently widowed resident of a future underground city, begins to question the virtual reality projected into the darkness around her.

Buenas Noches
Pedro usually earns his living drugging and robbing tourists, but upon meeting a girl who claims to have been cursed, he is confronted with the morality of his actions.

The King and His Three Sons
Three princes try to convince their father-king that they are worthy successors, but only one shall be the true heir.

Table of Contents

Cynder and the Magical Bucket

By Laurel Bucholz

THE BACKGROUND

Once upon a time, there was a young girl named Cynder who lived happily in a beautiful estate house. Things hadn't always been happy, though. She had been on a roller coaster ride over the past few years.

First, her mother passed away from a painful, degenerative disease. Then, her father remarried a terrible, horrible gold-digging bitch right before he up and had a deadly heart attack. So there Cynder was, quasi-orphaned, and then what does her step-mother-zilla do? Makes her a freaking indentured servant *in her own house* to her and her two horrible daughters! Cynder got used to being a doormat, because that's how things were, and she had never lived on her own, nor did she know any better. Things went on with her being an abused housemaid for a long damn time.

One day a letter came in the mail announcing the king's annual ball - but this ball was big news because the prince was going to choose his wife. Of course her step-mother-zilla didn't want to let Cynder go, and even tore up the dress her mice friends had painstakingly made her moments before it was time to leave. (You try sewing with hands the size of Donald Trump's, and threading a needle with bucked teeth...it blows...and it was all for nothing.) Cynder sat at home in her attic boohooing and feeling sorry for herself, (an old habit that thankfully she kicked soon after), and - bless her heart - her fairy godmother had heard her.

"Poor me is vanity, my dear. Cut your whinin' and get back to tryin'."

"Who are you?" Cynder asked, a surprised look on her tear-stained face.

"I'm Astrid, your fairy godmother, and I'm here to help you."

Cynder lashed out, "I don't need anymore mothers! All they ever do is die and make me clean...*Whaaa!!!!*"

"OK, honey child, that's enough of that *buuuullshit*. I'm gonna help you meet that prince, but you have to help me in exchange."

"*What?*" she asked in a hopeful voice.

"I'll give you a beautiful, expensive gown, some glass heels that are totally impractical to walk around in, and get you a ride to the party, BUT in return you have to let me shack up in your house for a while, and at some point you may have to lie and tell the king's guard that I'm not here...oh and I need you to hide this baggy of 'fairy dust' for me. Deal?"

"Uh, I don't understand. Why do you want to stay at my place? I don't think my step-mother-zilla would like that."

"I'll take care of her. And those 'sisters' of yours. Do we have a deal?"

Feeling happy for the first time in ages, Cynder replied ecstatically, "Uhhh, yeah! Sure! Take care of all this crap and you can stay as long as you like. I've gotta change something. *I can't live like this anymore!*"

"Booyah! *Mekka-lekka-hi-mekka-heini-ho!*" Astrid waved her magic wand and Cynder was suddenly wearing the sexiest 'come-hither-and-fuck-me' little black dress that anyone had ever seen. Ever. Not even a matter of opinion. Astrid gave her the glass heels she'd promised and put down a teleportation mat.

"OK girl. The teleportation device will only last until midnight. I know, I know - that's when the party gets going - but I don't have the power to make it last longer, so get home by then. I'm off to take care of your 'family problems.' Now - Go get you some man!"

Cynder stepped on the teleportation device and was beamed away to the palace. Prince Charming took one look at her and knew he was going to throw down his royalty card to try to hit that. He immediately fell in lust with her, ignoring all the other women in the room - except one that had a magnificently large booty, that Charming's eyes kept wandering over to all evening. In hindsight, this probably should have been a red flag....

Midnight struck, she left her shoe behind, blah blah blah. You know the rest. Let's fast forward, shall we?

So they got married. Cynder thought this would finally bring her happiness again. She never thought about how *maybe* it was a bad idea to marry a guy that she had literally only spent like five hours with, let alone knew what she really wanted out of life. It turned out that her and Prince Charming had nothing in common, and that the prince was kind of a 'bro' who wanted to sit around all day watching jousting, guzzling craft ale, and snorting enough 'fairy dust' to kill a small pony. Worse yet, any time Cynder had expressed wanting to write books, or work as a diplomat to keep the warring kingdoms at peace, or clean up the oceans that his kingdom had polluted, Charming would just say things like:

"War equals money, babe. Can't stop the machine. Why don't we just have some babies and live happily ever after? How's that sound?"

By the time he invoked his 'legal right' to 'Prima Nocte' - the royal right to sleep with other peasant women on their wedding nights, (EWW, I know...) - Cynder was done.

After many sleepless nights and reading a lot of self-help books, Cynder decided to sell her glass slipper on BayOfYee.com for a handsome sum, and move back into her beautiful estate house that was still being occupied by Astrid - who had claimed that her step-mom-zilla and sisters had been 'murdered by pirates.' Cynder didn't pry for further information.... Her divorce settlement from the prince also helped her to live freely and pursue her passions of writing and fighting for the oceans. She had learned many lessons over the course of that terrible period in her life, but the number one lesson was self-reliance.

THE NOW

So that brings us back to today, with Cynder, now a woman, living happily in her estate house. She was trying to complete her own self-help book, but had run into some writer's block, and Astrid - who was a reality TV junky - was no help, and neither were her mice friends who just defecated all over the place and never cleaned up after their damned selves. She needed this book to succeed. The profits would go to saving the ocean - a cause that was taking up all of her current fucks. She decided she needed to take a nice quiet walk in the forest. "Smell ya later!" she shouted as she left the house and headed towards the trail that ran to the ocean shores.

Not but five minutes into her journey had she ran into a situation that broke her peace.

"Bite my juicy apple! Bite it! You know you want to!" In the distance an old hunched-over woman who looked like a cliché of a witch was trying to get a sweet-looking young girl with dark raven hair to bite into her apple. The young girl clearly wasn't interested.

"I really don't want to. I'm terribly sorry. I'm just not hungry. Please stop forcing your apple in my face," she said politely, not wanting to hurt the woman's feelings despite the fact that the crone was clearly out of line.

The old woman screeched back, "You *will* eat my apple, Deary!" As she grabbed the back of the girl's head and tried to force the apple into her mouth, Cynder ran over. "What the HELL is going on here?!?" she demanded.

The old woman stopped and innocently replied in the sweetest grandmotherly voice, "Oh, I'm just trying to feed this apple to my daughter. It's good for her skin - makes her look like milk fresh from a cow's teat. Would you like to try some? Your skin's looking a bit drab, Deary - like a white lady with freckles who spent too much time at the beach. Why, you must be fifty-six, fifty-seven years old?"

"Bwa ha ha! I'd be jealous of my youth too, if I looked like someone from the cast of *The Golden Girls*. Now drop that apple and step away from the girl."

"Betty White?" the witch replied in a hopeful tone.

"Hmmm, more like...SOPHIA! With a bigger, uglier nose," Cynder retorted.

"She must eat this apple!" the old woman cried as she lunged back toward the girl, shoving the apple into her mouth. Cynder jumped forward, hip-checked the old biddy down to the ground, took the apple out of the girl's lodged-open jaws, and stuffed it into the granny's mouth. "*BITE MY JUICY APPLE LADY! BITE IT! YOU LIKE THAT?!*" The witch weakly attempted to swat at Cynder's arms, and wished for a brief moment that she had taken her calcium + D supplements like her doctor had ordered.

"Quit hitting yourself! Quit hitting yourself!" Cynder teased as she lightly slapped the old woman's face with her own hands. Her bones were just too feeble to fight off Cynder without snapping, so she gave up on struggling. Muffled by the apple in her mouth, she pleaded with

Cynder to stop.

"Peeeese sop. Peeaaas. Ah ooon't aaaake er eeee theeee affffle!"

Cynder removed the apple from the witch's mouth. "What's that? You won't make this young woman eat your apple?"

"Yes, I won't make her eat the apple. Please just get off of m…."

A small amount of the juices from the broken apple skin had run down her throat during the struggle, causing the old crone to drift off into a deep sleep.

"Oh, I can't thank you enough," the raven-haired girl gushed. "That was the third time that woman tried to hurt me. I don't care how good apples are for your skin. I just don't like them!" She fixed her bobbed hair and curtsied. "My name is Snow Yellow. Pleased to meet you."

"I'm Cynder." She took out her phone and started to dial a number. "Hold on a sec - Hi, is this the 'Home for People Past Their Prime'?….Great, I've got a witch here out at mile marker seven who has fallen and can't get up. Her teeth are brittle, so she needs only mushy food, and a long drawn-out game of checkers. She's under heavy sedation, and should be kept that way….Excellent! About how long?….OK, there'll be a girl named 'Snow Yellow' waiting here to sign off….Thanks, buh-bye!" Cynder put her phone back in her boot.

"The people from the old-folks' home will be here in an hour and they'll make sure this woman doesn't harm anyone ever again. Why was she trying to hurt you, Ms. Yellow?"

"Well, I think she thought I wanted to marry her son or something. You see, he's a prince and *maybe* she thought I would want to be queen and take her throne? I don't know. Truth is, I don't want to marry her son! I'm already in a relationship. Well, seven actually. I'm in love with seven men and I don't know who to pick! They're all so wonderful." Snow Yellow put her hands over her face and started to sob. "I'm sorry. I don't know why I'm telling you all of this."

"*Girrrrl.* I've been there. I was married to a prince once. You don't need any of that bullshit. If you love these seven other men, and this witch is getting locked up in the old folks' home, then you can do whatever you want. You're free to do as you please."

"But they're all dwarves! *Boo hoo hoo!* How can I love all seven of them? Society says I can only love one man and they have to be a *normal* size. Sniff sniff."

"Calm down. Come and sit over here on this rock. Let's break down your problem, shall we? A. Who cares if they're short? Short people have every reason to live. Don't base your life on a terrible Randy Newman song. So that takes care of their size. B. Why don't you tell me *why* you love them so I can understand the extent of your problem."

"Well, they're all just so wonderful. There's Achoo-y, Shy-Guy, Joyful, Mr. Curmudgeon, Drowsy, Dumb-ass and The Brain. Achoo-y is the best cleaner to have in the house. He takes the chore load off of me."

"Chores suck!"

"Yeah! They do! Shy-Guy teaches me to be more confident through watching him, and I admire his humbleness. Joyful cheers me up on bad days, and teaches me to be positive. He even has a song about it!" Snow started to whistle and sing, "*Always look on the light side of living, da dum, da dum, da dum, dummmm.* Isn't that catchy?"

"Ha ha, yeah - who doesn't love Monty Cobra?"

"Who?"

"Never mind. Go on."

"Mr. Curmudgeon can be a downer, but his sarcasm makes me laugh until my belly aches. I love it! I get so sick of being nice all the time. He's an outlet for my *dark side.*"

"We all have one of those, honey."

"Drowsy is the Best. Cuddler. Ever. I could never give him up. And, well, Dumb-ass may be dumb but," she looked around and lowered her voice, "he gives the greatest oral pleasure."

"You can't give that up. No way. *Givers are keepers.*"

"Exactly!" exclaimed Snow. "And finally there's The Brain. Do you know what a 'Sapiosexual' is?"

"Oh yeah, girl, I'm turned on by intelligence, too."

"You get me, Cynder! They're all special to me. How can I choose just one?"

"It sounds like you already live with these guys, right?"

"Yes, we live together."

"And they all know about each other then, I'm guessing?"

"Yes. They do. They seem OK with it."

"I'm not seeing a problem here. Your problem was over there. Now it's comatose. Wait - do these guys have jobs?"

"Oh yes, they're miners. They bring me jewels everyday."

"Yeah, still not seeing a problem here."

"But there are seven of them. And society says —"

"Fuck society. Do what makes *you* happy as long as you aren't hurting anybody. See this magical bucket?" Cynder pretended there was an invisible magical bucket in her hands. Snow nodded her head 'yes'. "Do you see any fucks in there?"

"No?" replied Snow, a little confused.

"Yes, you do. There are tons of fucks in my magical bucket. You know *why?*"

Snow shook her head 'no'.

"Because I don't go giving my fucks away on what society thinks I should be doing with my life."

Snow thought about it for a moment before declaring,"You're right! Jeez, Cynder! How can I ever repay you?" Snow pulled out a handful of precious gems from her cleavage and tried to hand them over.

Cynder waved her hand and shook her head. "Not necessary. My book is coming out soon, though. You could always purchase a copy on *Dinkle* for fourteen silver rupees if you feel inclined. The proceeds go to saving our ocean, and if you type in promo code #magicalbucket, you can get a 10% discount. It would make a great birthday gift for each of your dwarf boyfriends. Plus, it's for a good cause. Here's my card. Take care, Ms. Yellow. I'll be off now."

"I'll make sure to buy eight! Take care, Cynder. Thanks again!"

****

The forest was absolutely beautiful that day. Cynder had a stroke of inspiration that broke her writer's block, but just as quickly forgot what it was, as she ran into another distressed damsel weeping under a tree.

"Hey Chica - what's happening over here? Why are you crying on such a magnificent day?"

"I have no memory of the last year. I remember walking through a castle and pricking my finger on a spindle. When I woke up, this guy who calls himself 'Prince Pheelup' was trying to kiss me and I was in some strange bed. I don't remember consenting to any of it! Now my father says I have to *marry* this guy!"

"What? *Girrrl…that's fucked up!* No you don't!"

"I do, though….I could never disobey my father! I don't even know this Prince Pheelup guy! I mean, he's kind of cute and I have to admit that I can't stop thinking about his package in those tight little pants of his…and he does claim that nothing happened…." She bit her lip as she twirled her long blond tresses around her finger. "*He's yummy.*"

Cynder shook her head in annoyance before forcefully asking, "How long have you known this guy?"

"Well, we walked together once upon a dream, and then there was this one time we sang a duet in the forest, and then just that morning when I woke up."

"So you've barely hung out three times?"

"Mmm, yeah. I guess you could say that." Her cheeks reddened with awkward embarrassment.

"Did you feel violated downstairs when you woke up?"

"Downstairs?" She shook her head at Cynder, obviously not understanding the reference.

"Your vajay? Your *tiny princess* down there. Did you feel any pain down there the morning you woke up?"

"Ohhhhhh. Well, noooooo. My royal virginity still seems to be in tact. And he did say that he was told to kiss me because of some 'curse' that was put on me."

"That sounds like a load of bullshit!"

"*Right?*" agreed the girl.

Cynder reached into her satchel and pulled out a small bottle of red nail polish. "What's your name sweetie?"

"Beauty," she stated demurely.

"Of course it is….Beauty, give me your hand." Beauty reluctantly held out her hand as Cynder placed the bottle in her palm and closed her fingers around it. She looked straight into her eyes. "Beauty, this nail polish is specially made to know if you have been drugged or not. Specifically, *roofied.* While you're wearing it, you can dip your fingers into any drink you're given. If the color turns green, *DON'T DRINK THE DRINK.* Do you understand?"

"Uh huh."

"Now, Prince Pheelup sounds like he may or may not be a skeezy rapist. I like giving people the benefit of the doubt, though. So, since you're kinda into this guy, you should spend more time with him before committing to marriage. I did what you're about to do before. Three short encounters doth not a marriage make. Trust me. Does all of this sound reasonable?"

"Yes, but my father—"

"Ahhhh. Yes. Your father. Hmmm. How can we fix the problem of your father acting like it's still the fourteenth century?" Cynder clasped her fist to her chin and pretended to look as if she were pondering the problem for about three seconds.

"I've got it! Do you see this magical bucket?" Cynder again mimed an invisible magical bucket in her arms. "Do you see any fucks in this magical bucket?"

Beauty shook her head with a very unsure 'no.'

"Yes, you do. There are tons of fucks in this magical bucket because I do what I want with my life and don't give a fuck about what my irrational father wants me to do. You catch my drift?"

Beauty's eyes widened while nodding her head with a knowing 'yes.'

"Great. Now, do you have anyone you can go and stay with for a few months or even a year? That way you have some time to actually date this Pheelup prince?"

Beauty perked up. "Yes, I do! I can go stay at my Godmother Malignant's cottage just up the road."

"Great! Go home. Tell your father that you refuse to marry a stranger, and that you're going to stay with your Godmother Malignant - who sounds like a badass by the way. Malignant. Whew. Wouldn't want to mess with a name like that. She sounds like a tumor! Ha ha ha —"

"SHE'S NOT A TUMOR!" shouted Beauty indignantly.

"Of course she's not! Go to your Godmother Malignant who's not a tumor's house and tell her you need to stay with her for a while. Don't take 'no' for an answer, OK?"

Beauty heaved a sigh of relief and smiled. Her name stood up to her exquisiteness. "Thank you. I don't even know you and you've helped me so much."

Cynder pulled out her card and handed it to her. "Name's on the card. I've got to be going now. My book comes out soon. Buy it as repayment on *Dinkle* for only fourteen silver rupees! Type in the promo code #magicalbucket to get 10% off. Proceeds go to saving our oceans. Oh, and Beauty?"

"Yes?"

"Get yourself some hobbies. Dudes aren't everything. See you around." She winked at her as she went about her walk.

****

The day's light was fading and Cynder hoped she could derive some inspiration from a lovely sunset at the beach - as well as check on her cause. As she approached the shore, she saw a large boulder about three feet out. On it was an outline of a mermaid. When she got closer, she saw that the mermaid was skipping some thingamajiggers along the water as if they were stones while muttering something along the lines of:

"Stupid fuckin' fish tail. No legs. Gross home. Give up my voice to live with some random strange hottie or live here in the pollution? What the hell kind of choice is that? Fucking fuck! Fuckity fuck!"

"*Whoa, girrrl.* What seems to be the problem here? I've got some sake in my bag. Would you like a swig?"

The mermaid turned around, startled. "Oh. I'm sorry. I — I didn't realize anyone was here. Please don't tell my father I was using such foul language. It'll be just one more headache for me." She huffed and blew her red bangs out of her face.

"I don't give a fuck what language you use, hun. Words are meant to express. Did you know that cursing is scientifically proven to lower levels of stress? That's a fact. Curse away!"

"*Noooo,* I didn't fucking know that. Why the *fuck* would

I? I don't fucking get to study science. I'm stuck in this shit-ridden ocean, day in, day out. Fuck me! Have you seen the state of my fucking home lately? I came up here around noon to get the fucking sludge out of my body and have been doing it all fucking afternoon." She pressed her index finger to her right nostril and blew black tar out of the left. It stuck to the rock like slime. "See! Fucking disgusting! And look at this shit!" The mermaid held out her forearm to reveal a strange discolored rash that was visibly bubbling - even from shore. "It's fucking gross. And fuck-off painful. Fuck! Fuck! Fuckity fuck!" She tossed another thingamajigger and it sunk after three skips.

"OK, you don't need to curse *that* much, girl. Maybe save them up for a bigger stress release."

Cynder waded through the water, climbed up on the rock and sat next to her. She pulled out some ointment from her satchel. "Here. Put this on your arm. It'll deaden the pain for a while. It's waterproof, too. You just need to reapply it every four hours or so."

"Thanks. My name's *EEEEADFADFEEEEEEEEEEAAAOOUUEEE!!!*"

Cynder quickly covered her ears to avoid becoming deaf from the sound of Mer-language.

"Wow!" Cynder replied, waiting for the ringing in her ears to stop. "That's, uh…beautiful….Do you happen to have an English name?"

"Name's Areola…I think…at least, that's what the hot guy I rescued last week called me after I resuscitated him. His beautiful eyes opened while I was leaning over him. He took his first breath and said, 'I can see you're Areola'." She sighed. "It's a nice name, don't you think? Anyways, I'd shake your hand, but, I wouldn't want you to catch whatever I've got."

"Uh, an areola is the ring around your nip — nevermind. You don't have anything, honey. It's the chemicals from the kingdom that are causing your arm to bubble like that. I've already submitted a petition to the king to get it cleaned up."

"Well, I can't handle this for much longer! You know I may have to go and live with him if my ocean doesn't get cleaned up soon."

She started to sing.

"*You want thingamajiggers? I got them off a Bentley! I've got whose-its and whats-its from world wars!*"

"What will I do with my things up here? I went to ask the sea witch if she could give me some legs, and do you know what that sea-cow said? She said I'd have to give her my voice! What the *hell* kind of trade is that? Basically I can trade my legs and dignity so I can walk around up here with some strange dude or I can die slowly of toxic sludge like my father, the tyrant, wants me to. Ugh. My father, the king. Don't get me started on him."

Areola started to sing again.

"*Bet you on sand, they understand that they shouldn't disrespect their daughters. My dad's a villain. I'd like to kill him. Ready to staaaaaaaab—*"

SLAP!!! Cynder smacked Areola hard across her face.

"OW!!"

"That was a reality check. This is no time for singing! Your voice is beautiful — keep it. They most certainly do disrespect their daughters on sand! As for your thingamajigs and whose-its and whats-its?" Cynder turned around and looked at the shore. She squinted and pointed to a random spot.

"Do you see that bucket there in the sand, near that crazy old seagull? I left my magical bucket on shore because I didn't want the rest of my fucks escaping into the water."

Areola looked at her like she was crazy.

"I don't see any bucket."

"Just roll with it. There's a magical bucket I left onshore. Do you see any fucks inside?"

"What? I don't see anything except a seagull smoking a pipe."

Cynder breathed a heavy sigh. "Let's try this again. There's a magical bucket there. Usually I have tons of fucks inside, but right now that magical bucket is half-empty, because most of my fucks I had have gone to caring for your ocean. I am deeply concerned about the future of your home, as it affects all of us. *Now*, let's see *your* magical bucket."

"I have a snarf-blatt? Does that count?"

"No. Hold up your arms and pretend you have a bucket." She grabbed Areola's arms while carefully avoiding her rash. "Are there any fucks in your bucket?"

"Yes? Is that the right answer?"

"Yes, it is! Because you don't give any fucks about stuff and things. Your fucks are reserved for your home and your body. That's the important stuff. Do you get it now?"

"Kind of…."

"What do you care about?"

"The cute guy I rescued?"

"Nope. Try again.

"Stuff and things?"

"Wrong! You care about your home, your independence, and your value as a mer-person!"

Sitting up straight while jutting her breasts out, Cynder caught a glimpse of how Areola got her name before she replied, "I do! You're right!"

"I've got some good news for you, too. I'm about to finish my book and the profits will be used to clean up your home, so I need you to hang tight for a bit longer. No shacking up with strange dudes. And no giving out unnecessary fucks."

"So, I can't sleep with the hottie?"

"NOT those kind of fucks…but sure, you can do whatever you want. What I meant was…caring. Don't go caring about things that aren't worth your time."

"So, I don't have to give up my voice?"

"No."

"And I don't have to move in with a stranger, live as a mute, and have my tail horrifically ripped in two?"

"No."

"And my friends won't be eaten anymore?"

"That's probably still going to happen. Especially if they're crabs or flounders. People think those species are particularly delicious. Just hope people don't suddenly develop a taste for mermaid, which would be quasi-cannibalism, but I wouldn't worry too much about that unless there's an apocalypse or something."

Areola looked traumatized.

"Well, look at that - the sun's almost set. Here, take my card. Name's Cynder. Buy my book for fourteen silver rupees on *Dinkle* if you want your home cleaned up faster. Promo code #magicalbucket for 10% off. Tell your friends!"

"Thanks? *I think...*" Areola tossed the rest of her thingamajiggers into the ocean and dove in.

****

By now it had grown quite dark as Cynder made her way back home to finish the end of her book. A nice glass of scotch would clear out any remaining writer's block. The forest was serene at night with little to fear, and illuminated by the light of the full moon. Her peaceful walk was suddenly broken by the sound of a man and woman arguing. The woman was standing on her balcony about ten feet above the ground, and the man was high up on his magic carpet next to her ledge.

"Come on, *baby. Let me show you my world.* Slippery, sparkling - it's *distended.*" Jafink waggled his eyebrows twice at her.

"Ugh! For the last time, I'm not interested in seeing your '*world*.'"

"Ahh, Princess - *when was the last time you let your penis flytrap decide?*"

"I hate it when you call me princess and don't call my vag a—"

"I've got a fantastic *point* for you to view. *No one can tell me 'no'! Come on,* just a blow j—"

"You're dreaming, Jafink."

"Last month you said you wanted a carpet ride, baby!"

"Ugggh. Yes. A carpet ride home! And now that you're here it's crystal clear that YOU'RE A TOTAL DOUCHE!

"*Jaaaaz.* Jazzy baby. *Jaz!* Which position do you like? Over? Sideways? Under? How about we go up to the sky and have *a real magic carpet ride?*" He humped the air for added effect. "Your father will never know!"

"I SAID '*NO*'!"

Jafink lunged forward and tried to pull Jaz onto his floating rug.

"No! Get off of me! *HELP! Mr. Fluffers!*" She whistled, and from the balcony lunged a giant Bengal tiger onto Jafink, knocking him off the carpet and down to the ground where he landed right at Cynder's feet.

"Are you OK up there, lady?" she called up to the balcony.

"Oh, yes. I can take care of myself," Jaz stated quite assuredly while she fixed the puff of her baby-blue hammer pants.

Cynder patted her fist twice on her chest and motioned to the woman. "Respect."

Jaz mirrored her back, and replied, "Stay safe down there with that *creep.*"

"I've got this."

Jaz gave a knowing head motion and went into her palace, her tiger and Jafink's carpet following behind her. "Come on, Mr. Fluffers. Let's get ready for a real carpet ride."

Back on the ground, Jafink writhed in pain from a snapped knee and a nasty bump on the head. "Help me, please," he said through gritted teeth. "Call my monkey Apu."

"Oh, hell no!"

"OK, then Genie."

"Those are the lamest pickup lines I've ever heard."

"Please help me, arrggh, *it hurts!*"

"Gee, let me check my magical bucket. Hmmm. Nope. I've got no fucks in here for dudes who don't understand that **NO MEANS NO!**"

"Did you see what she was wearing? Midriff showing and all that cleavage? She was asking for it!"

Suddenly, a tall, dark, handsome man appeared from the shadows. Every curve of his ripped muscles and cocoa butter skin was exposed under the moonlight, as he was wearing only a vest for a top, and some hammer pants.

"Apu is mine, Jafink! You were warned to leave my lady alone! I caught the tail end of your disgusting conversation with Jaz."

"Mr. Abs! You filthy little street rat! I've been looking for you everywhere!"

"You're going to be sorry you finally found me." He cracked his knuckles. "*Very sorry*...Oh! I didn't see you there. Hello, miss. Did this asshole try to hurt you, too?"

Cynder couldn't stop staring at Mr. Abs' pecs and washboard stomach. "No, nooo. I can take care of myself - just like your lady up there."

"She's pretty special, ain't she? So smart and beautiful. I love how independent she is - and funny too - people don't realize that. She honestly makes me a better man. I'm so lucky she fell in love with *me*. I can't wait to share a whole new world with her."

"See, when you say it, it doesn't sound skeezy - it sounds romantic. You two are very lucky to have each other."

"Thanks. I'd better take care of this shit head," he put his foot over Jafink's mouth, covering his creepy child-molester mustache, "and then head up there to see her. It's our anniversary. I'm taking her on a magic carpet ride just like the one we took on our first date."

"That's sweet. I better be off then. It was nice meeting you." Cynder blushed when she shook Mr. Abs' hand good-bye.

As she left, listening to the sound of Jafink getting the shit kicked out of him, Cynder had a small fantasy about a future with a guy like Mr. Abs, but she didn't entertain those thoughts for too long. It gave her great pleasure to run into another woman who knew where to place her fucks - especially after the day she had had. She wondered why so many women were obsessed with men. She knew she used to be one of them, but was proud of how far she had come since the days of Prince Charming. Now, she finally had inspiration for the end of her book.

****

Not but a mile away from her home, she ran into a familiar face.

"*Sup*, Cynder! Been looking for you *everywhere*, girl! I even got lost looking for you. I haven't seen a 7-Eleven in like twenty minutes."

Cynder took one look at him - unkempt beard, piercings, black plastic glasses, in obvious need of a hair cut - and knew she wasn't doing this bullshit again. She had had a long day dealing with everyone's problems and was in no mood for more shit.

"Charming, we're DIVORCED! *Remember?!* I find you repulsive on all levels. Can't help you. Byeeeeeeeee!" she cried as she attempted to slink away.

"Awww, *babe*. You were always good at playing hard to get! Remember that time you left your shoe at the ball. Ha! Classic Cyn."

Cynder rolled her eyes. "Yeah, 'bro' - um - what the *hell* are you doing here? The restraining order was still in effect last I checked."

"Oh, yeah. Totally is. I just thought you were joking, babe. Everybody loves '*The Charm*'!"

"Ugh! Nobody likes '*The Charm*' and please stop calling yourself that. Did your father sign that Order of Royal Decree to clean up the oceans yet? I got 100,000 signatures for the petition just like he asked. You said you would make sure he signed it last month."

"Aw, shit. Babe. Totally flaked on that."

"I'm *real* shocked. Hey! You see this magical bucket?" She mimed a magical bucket in her arms. "Do you see any fucks in this magical bucket?"

Charming got super excited. "Yeah, baby! I see what you're throwing down. I've got some fucks for you, too!"

31

"**NO**! There are **ZERO** fucks in this magical bucket for you. They are all *MY* fucks and they're going to clean up the oceans that your stupid kingdom helped to pollute! Plus, you STILL reek of vaping and over-priced craft ale. I do believe there's a sing-a-long bar about a mile from here that way." She pointed in the direction of the very steep and incredibly harrowing town cliff. "**NO FUCKS FOR YOU!**"

Charming started walking backwards in the direction she had pointed. "Hey, thanks! I really love sing-a-long bars! That's fantastic. I knew you still loved me, Cyn! You sure you don't want to come with me? I can do a mean version of Radiohead's "Creep". I swear I sound just like Thom Yorke now. Come and check me ou- *AHHHHHHHHHHH!*"

SPLAT

"Good riddance," she thought to herself, and smiled as she saw her house up ahead.

She walked straight into the house, sat down at her computer, finished the final page of her book, and sent the file off to her editor. As she climbed into bed and her body relaxed under the cool sheets, she heard the floor creak at the doorway. It was Astrid.

"Cyn? Are you still awake? Something's really been bugging me lately."

Cynder sighed, still lying flat. "What *is it* Astrid?"

"Well, there's this prince, and I think I'm falling in lo—"

"Ugggghhhh!" Exasperated, Cynder shot up and stared directly at Astrid while speaking through her teeth. "Seriously?! Do you see this magical bucket?!"

THE END

UPDATE *Charm Yourself - A Guide to Prioritizing Your Fucks* was last seen at #3 on the *Fairyland Times* Best Seller list. So far, it's raised over six billion silver rupees, allowing for a massive ocean cleanup, and Areola never had to move in with any strange dudes.

Inspiration
Inspired by a man named Walt who corrupted my childhood, and all the lovely ladies out there who need a reminder that having a man does not equate happiness, nor determine your value.

About the Author
Laurel Bucholz thinks too much, but would appreciate it if others would think more. This is her first published short story. She periodically dabbles in comedy, voice work, writing, and performing and can be contacted via email at imnotlaurel@yahoo.com for collaboration. She has a new book coming out in January 2017 called '7 Billion to Go', a humorous take on the state of the world, which will be illustrated for adults. For more information, check out www.facebook.com/7billiontogo. Let the dabbling continue! Thank you Shannon, your love and support made this possible.

The One Who Bleeds

By Nick Vaky

I am running through the grass slopes: fields that incline and decline over and over for miles, and where the thin green strands are sometimes as high as I am. The grass slaps against my legs while I barrel through it all. It hits my eyes but I go faster, so fast that I shoot out of the fields, an unstoppable force. All the tension of my muscles is set loose and I am running through the vast emptiness where nothing much grows: the place I call home.

When I run, I bleed. I reach open country and the wind hits me hard and stinging and wonderful and the cold is sweet and clean and fills my nostrils. My neck muscles strain. My hind legs kick away from my front legs in perfect synchronicity, and my pores drip blood.

This is when I feel alive. Eyes fixed on the horizon, every muscle flexing and moving, breath steady and deliberate. The world blurs and the blood covers my beautiful gray skin, all sticky but not uncomfortable. The cool air of the northern country blows onto me and sends my mane flying wild. I run. I bleed. Time is a vortex that is at once eternal and fleeting.

I slow my sprint to a canter and let the world slide back into clarity. Here, where the snow meets the grass slopes, the earth is flat and hard and the climate calms me.

I stop, even though my legs feel unnatural standing still. I kneel down and bite into snow that melts on my tongue as I chew. I find a patch of hard dirt to bend my front legs down on and I sleep in the hope that I will dream of running, running through a flat land devoid of trees, devoid of hills or brush, a land where there are no grass slopes, a land where I eat the air and drink the rain, a land that stretches on forever and ever and where I never need stop.

****

I wake to a tightening on my mouth. A strap wraps all the way around, holding my jaw shut. Then I feel a sharp pain in my back. All around me in the darkness are the creatures that walk on two legs: men. How many are there? It's too dark and they are too many. I rear up and kick, standing on two legs like they do. I bear back down on one of the men from a great height, smash my front legs onto his chest, and crush his frail bones.

More sharp pain on my hind legs and I kick back into one of these creatures. I hear him scream in agony and it gives me pause. They are all yelling and hollering now. I see the sharp sticks they hold out to protect themselves. They have encircled me.

Another rope slides heavy around my neck. The men yank me down hard, four or five of them pulling together is enough to make me fall. I crash down onto my side and hit dirt mixed with snow. Ropes around my legs, I try to flail and kick but the men pull the bindings tight, on my front legs first, then my hind legs. I'm helpless.

A tall man, much cleaner than the others, reveals himself in flickering torch light. The hoard of two-legged creatures pull tighter on the ropes—constricting pain—knots tightening as the tall man approaches. He bends down, looks into my eyes, and reaches out for my torso.

****

The king touches the horse on the chest, and feels it breathing. The fear of this animal is so much like the fear of the men he has conquered that it makes him smile. The king pulls his hand away and sees that it is true: his hand is stained red. A horse that sweats blood. His grandfather told him the stories of the animals: horses that are faster than any other, horses that sweat blood when they run. His grandfather, the greatest king their country has ever known, told him that a king with a northern horse would be unstoppable on the battlefield. No king in a hundred years has ridden on a horse that bleeds and here is such a horse, captured and lying in the mud.

"Picture the terror of the enemy when they see your king riding a horse covered in blood!" he yells to the men surrounding him.

"Aye, Your Grace, utter terror," says a soldier gritting his teeth and holding out a spear, staring into the eyes of the angry beast.

"Pull him up and take him to camp," the king

commands. "We ride south at first light."

****

The king dreams of conquering westward. He dreams of stabbing men in the throat and mowing down companies, trampling them, and grinding their bones under the hooves of his new horse. He dreams of riding to the ocean that their kingdom has never seen. He dreams of an ocean of blood.

****

They make a slow pace back from the northern country. The horse that bleeds is stubborn and reluctant to move. The soldiers have to drag him, sometimes ten men together, over hills and through mud.

I will break him in due time, thinks the king as the horse kicks up dust and pulls against his bindings.

When they reach the kingdom, instead of entering through the back passage that leads directly to the castle, the entourage enters through the city streets to show the people what they have brought back from the north. The people clap and cheer for the king and his new northern horse: his prize.

A child from the crowd, a boy, is so infatuated with the animal that he sneaks his way through the lines of men and touches the horse. Up close the boy can see the horse is tired and hungry. The boy has no food but he pets the horse's mane and hair. He looks into the eyes of the horse and whispers to him.

The king sees the boy touching his horse, whispering to his horse. The entourage stops. The king orders his men to cart the boy to the dungeons, not because he wants to but because he must, to show the people that this is the horse of kings, not of peasant children. The crowd is reluctant to learn this lesson; whispers and rumbles of anger bubble up inside the mob. The king squelches the unrest by calling out to the grieving crowd that misfortune is deserved on the heads of the unworthy.

Once on the castle grounds, the horse is taken to the stables and the king is beset by all manner of ministers asking for decisions on the water conditions in the city, the planning of a festival, the storage of grain reserves, how to handle the marauding barbarians from the west. He answers their questions and issues pronouncements, but all the while his mind is thinking of riding the steed, the only thing he's been thinking of since the horse was caught.

****

The next morning, the stable master is trying to get the horse out of the enclosure when the king comes down to see him. The horse that bleeds has dug in. As hard as the stable master pulls, the horse cannot be moved. A testament to this is the twelve-year-old stable hand writhing on the hay-covered ground with an open head wound. His attempt to pull out the horse led to nothing more than a slip on the stone and a hard knock to the head.

The king enters to this mayhem and is displeased. "Why is that horse still inside?" he asks plainly, firmly.

"Your Grace!" The stable master tries to kneel and the

horse kicks up, forcing the stable master to stand again and pull back on the reins to steady the strong animal. "The 'orse did rear up and kick the boy in the 'ead. I called for nurse, an' now I'm tryin' to calm the creature, to git 'im out."

The king stares at the pools of blood matted with yellow hay.

"Don't worry 'bout the boy, Your Grace. 'Ell be fine."

"I want this horse out and ready to be broken no later than noon," the king declares.

****

The king eats in the great hall, and as he eats, he listens to the minister of agriculture dryly explain a type of insect found in nearby crops. The minister is describing, in painstaking detail, the physiological properties of the insect. The king tries his best to glean the point of what the expert is elucidating—but he cannot, and the king is not a man who has the patience for such long-winded reports. So, he sends the expert, with his valuable information, away.

At noon, the stable master comes up covered in sweat.

" 'E won't budge, Your Grace. I tried to pull 'im with four men and . . . the 'orse don't move."

The king considers hanging the stable master but instead says, "Try five men."

"Aye, five men," the stable master says and looks to the ground.

"Something else?" the king asks, glaring.

"The boy, Your Grace . . . is dead."

"Yes." The king frowns. "Tell me when the horse is out.

I want to see him run."

"Aye, Your Grace." The stable master bows and goes off to find five men.

At around four o'clock they call the king down to the grass courtyard that is adjacent to the stables. The king watches with a frown as horse that bleeds stands, won't run. The king watches the stable master tire himself out whipping the horse, the stubborn horse that stares into the eyes of the king, unafraid. A whip cracks on the horse's back, and his muscles never so much as twitch from the pain, let alone move of their own volition.

The king has no choice now—the stable master is dragged away by guards and taken to the dungeons that stretch beneath the castle.

"You're in change of the stable now," the king tells a nearby servant who simply quivers his lip and nods. "Try bribing the beast with apples."

The apples don't work. Whipping the horse doesn't work. Sending him out with the other horses doesn't work. The horse that bleeds won't run. The king cannot sleep. Every dream he has is about the horse that bleeds. Every waking moment his mind wanders to riding and how the horse won't move. The king tries to ride the other horses in the royal stables but all it does is incite his desire for the horse that bleeds.

Two government ministers beat down the door of the great hall. The war minister asks the king what to do about the barbarians laying waste to the villages while the minister of agriculture tries his best to present statistics on the dwindling food stores, statistics which he has been entreating the king to listen to for over a month. The king

40

doesn't hear, doesn't want to, all he can do is mumble, "Crush them with our army and grow more food." Any other questions from the men prompts nothing more than an apathetic wave.

Every day, at an earlier time than the previous one, the king leaves the great hall, traverses the steps down to the castle's courtyard, and walks to the stables to stare at the strong, stubborn horse that will not yield to him. He stands in the royal stables amongst the hay, and when he's sure there's no one watching, when he's sure his guards are outside and out of view, he cries.

****

I know the horse because he's bigger than the others. I know this human because everyone calls him "Your Grace." His clothes are clean and he smells like flowers and citrus. Every day when I come to the stables looking for food, Your Grace is staring at the northern horse and crying. He looks ridiculous, sobbing with a gleaming hat on his head. I wait under the hay until Your Grace wipes his eyes and leaves the stable.

When the human is gone, I come out and continue searching the ground for scraps of food. I sniff the floor, darting left then right. My tail drags along the cool stone. I feel the northern horse with his long face and sad eyes staring at me and I let him gawk because I know the look in his face. It's hunger. I'd recognize that look anywhere. I have it in my bones. My family has it in their blood. We pass it down through generations.

I've been watching this horse for months, since he

41

arrived. First, they beat him, then they bribed him, and now they are depriving him of food and still he won't do what they want. He is noble—but dumb. The poor, stupid animal is too large to be crafty like us. A smart animal never reveals his worth to the humans. Small, useless scum is what we are: pests that they kick away and sometimes kill. And yet I can crawl through every wall and know every corner of their castle. Maybe not so noble but certainly not so—I notice a scrap of apple wedged in a crack in the stone floor. I gnaw at it with my front teeth and am able to pull out some of the meat. The rest of the fruit is too far down. I keep trying to get at it and scrape my teeth on stone. Yes, I know hunger.

Food has been going scarce for a long while now. When the rats are desperate, something rotten is going on.

I look back at the horse and see that he's stopped staring at me and is now staring at the hay. He wants it. Needs it. So I oblige, bite down on a tuft of straw, drag it to his stall, climb the short wooden door and drop it in. No sense in both of us starving.

His big, ugly mouth chews and slops up the strands of yellow, all the while staring at me. Watching big animals eat is disgusting, but it does remind me I'm hungry. As if I ever need reminding.

There is a patch of rotting wood behind the hay-bale; it leads to a burrow that goes under the courtyard, from which there is a system of tunnels that span in all directions. I can run into the city or up into the castle through the dungeons. What little food can be found in the city is being fought over by the others. I head to the castle.

Crawling through the darkness of the dungeons I can

see the humans squinting and groping in their cages, but none of them see me. Months ago this was an excellent place to find food: you could take a bite right from the plate of a man and he would never know you were there. But lately the humans have stopped feeding these ones.

I crawl up the wet part of the wall and through a hole in the ceiling that leads to the wine cellar. Above that are the kitchens. In the past I'd stop and eat in either of these places, but recently the quality of the food has been lacking. I've found the only clean food comes from the plate of the human they call Your Grace.

Above the kitchens is a room with high ceilings and a large table. Through my favorite crack in the stone wall I spy the cloth-draped, redwood table covered with golden bowls and cups. The legs of the humans go past and I smell so much food I can barely identify it all: meat covered in salt and cumin . . . potatoes . . . fish and onions. The other rats fear the bustle of this place. What they don't know is all it requires to get the excess of these nobles is a modicum of patience.

"Where is the bread?" It's the voice of Your Grace.

"The wheat fields were burned last week, Your Grace," says the human sitting next to him.

A fist slams down and causes fruits to roll off the table, landing a tail's length away from me—two shiny grapes, so close I can almost taste them. I resist the urge to run out and snatch them up. It would be easy enough to grab the fruit, but it would be easier still for one of the humans to stomp me.

"Tell them to rip the teeth out of the barbarians to teach them what it means to go hungry!" Your Grace yells.

"It was not the barbarians, Your Grace. I ordered the wheat burned."

"Why would you do such a thing?"

"I needed to act, Your Grace, lest we lose all the crops. The insects are spreading faster than I can track them."

I see the legs of a serving boy walking past the table.

"Insects?" Your Grace asks.

"Yes, between these insects and the invaders, there is no food left for the people to eat. The livestock is dying of hunger because the wheat is gone and the insects have spread through the dying animals. I cannot control the spread. Every day another crop is affected."

The serving boy with thin legs takes the unfinished plate of Your Grace and his companion. The humans at the table have moved on to eating sweets, fruit, and milk pudding.

"By all estimates, in a month, the people will be dying of starvation in the streets."

The boy with the plates goes exactly where I expect he will, out the door in the back of the room. I head into the wall to make my way, unseen, to the back door though a twisting tunnel of gaps and cracks. I can still hear the vibrations of Your Grace's voice through the stone bricks.

"Kill the horses."

"Your Grace?"

"You say we need food? Kill the horses and use the meat however you like."

"Your Grace, I am not certain how wise . . .."

I come out of the wall into the back room of the dining hall, a small room filled with wooden troughs and buckets. I wait behind a bucket as the boy dumps the plates of Your Grace into a large trough and turns back to the hall. The voices from the hall are muffled but I still hear.

"Of course, keep any military animals alive, but I'm finished with all the horses in the royal stables. They make me sick to look at. They can be ground up and fed to whomever you see fit. I suggest the army."

"Certainly, Your Grace."

My nose is fixed on the wooden trough filled with potatoes and soggy meat. I am about to dart out of hiding when the boy reverses himself and puts his arms into the trough, pulling out handfuls of waste food and shoving as much of the slop as he can into his mouth. Fist over fist, forcing it in his mouth as quickly as he can, dribbling it down his chin and trying his best not to get it on his serving clothes. Hungry eyes on this one, too. Hungry eyes on everyone lately.

The boy wipes his mouth and leaves through the swinging wooden door.

With caution, and one eye on the entrance, I make my way to the trough.

"Except for the northern horse . . . he will be on my table."

I stop. The northern horse.

"I want to eat him raw. I will finally make him bleed for me."

I look into the trough and picture the head of the beautiful northern horse floating in the slop. It seems I'll be eating ground up pieces of horse soon.

What does it matter? I tell myself. Meat is meat. The dumb horse should have run.

I dig my back feet into the rim of the trough and lean my body down, stretching to eat from the waste bin of

Your Grace. I eat like that until I'm full, wander to a crack in the wall, and fall asleep.

****

I am in a—cage. My family is all around me, stacked on top of me. Packed in so tight in such a small space. I am against the edge of the cage, my body and fur pressed against thick strips of irons. Feet and claws scratch my head and I claw and scratch at the head underneath me. I try to move between the hot bodies of my brothers and sisters, but I cannot. Then I feel it under my feet: water rising up slowly and deliberately. The squeals of my brothers and sisters turn into bubbling gurgles. The water reaches my nose and pours into my mouth, filling my stomach.

****

I wake up inside the wall, dry and alive. The total darkness of a self-made hovel wraps me up and cools down the heat of my fear. All the food I ate sits heavy inside me. I can still hear the squealing of my dreams, and I replay these images of being trapped and drowning with my family. Nervously I begin to chew on the wall, gnawing on stone and grinding down my teeth.

"Kill the horses," Your Grace said. Kill the horses he loves so much?

I imagine it's the horses drowning next to me and they scream just like rats do.

He won't do it.

The slop turns over inside my body; I need to drink.

I run one thousand tail lengths forward, and then run a thousand more straight down past the kitchens, into the wine cellar. Down here the squealing from my dreams only gets louder. I find a leaking cask and lap at the red liquid pooling into the cracks of stone. This wine tastes sour, old. Well, I am lapping it up off a dirty stone floor after all.

I stop drinking and listen. The squeals are above me, not in my head.

Best to stay away.

But it's so loud and it sounds like—family.

I run back into the wall and up seventy-six tail lengths. When I peer out into the kitchens, my skull reverberates with cries of pain and terror.

"God in heaven they are loud," laughs a human with sleeves rolled up, both hands in a wooden barrel of water. They call this one Cook.

"You *are* drowning them," says the serving boy.

"How can they squeal so loud in the water?" asks Cook.

"Don't know. You sure no one will be able to tell its rat?" asks the serving boy.

Rat?

"You know what rat tastes like?" asks Cook.

"Don't know," says the boy. "But I can't . . .."

"No. You KNOW what rat tastes like." Cook has a good laugh at this. "None of the servants have said a thing thus far, so it's safe to say—" The squeals stop. Cook smiles and even from my hiding place I can see his pointed black teeth. "—No one can tell. Now shut up and dump a few more in. These are dead."

The cook pulls two of my sisters from the barrel and holds their drowned and dripping bodies out for the serving

47

boy to see. I don't stay to see what he does with them.

Back into the wall, down past the wine cellar, through the dungeons. I breeze past the blind humans in their cages. No family, anywhere, none in the walls, none in the dungeons, how long have they all been missing? I didn't know—servants have been eating rats for how long?

I'm at the junction. I can go into the city but the people there are hungrier than those in the castle and the rats—no, there are no rats in the city anymore.

I sit. Breathe. There's a back entrance to the castle that leads to the forest. I can scale the wall of the dungeons and exit through the stables, then—the stables.

Damn.

I scale the wall and come out behind the mound of hay in the corner, poking my head out of strands of dried feed. The moon, a full circle, shines bright in the window, illuminating me. I go to the far stall first.

On top of the wood that boxes a horse in, I use my head to flick up the latch and the short wooden door swings open. The small brown horse inside stirs and reels back from me. The animal, instead of exiting, pushes back against the wall of his stall, snorting loudly at me, scraping hooves on stone to push away. This dumb animal doesn't know a golden axe is coming for him.

I move to the next stall, climb the door and release the latch. The horse inside barely glances at the open door and instead continues to lap up water from a dirty pail in the corner.

Down the line, I unhook the latches of the big dumb animals and not one will accept their freedom. Until I reach the stall of the northern horse. I unlatch his door and the gray beast bounds up as fast as any animal I have ever seen. The northern horse stands tense with nervous energy, hunger in his eyes, breathing fast and heart beating like a rat's. I turn and he follows, out the open door of the stable and into the night air, walking together: the last rats.

I lead him in the moonlight across the grass courtyard. Atop the walls that encircle us, humans slowly survey the land beyond the castle. I can only hope that they don't look our way: the eyes of humans are weak but the northern horse is large and the moon is bright.

Past the courtyard and through an alcove is the back gate, guarded by a fat sleeping human leaning inside the awning. Don't know the name of this one. In the past, before food became so scarce, he would fall asleep covered in crumbs, leaving chunks of bread around him to be devoured by as many as four of us at a time. We would sometimes eat the crumbs directly off his chest without causing him to so much as flutter his eyelids. If his breathing wasn't so loud you would think the poor, fat fellow was dead.

I crawl past fat legs to the crosshatched iron that bars the back gate. I am able to sneak through the holes in the iron that lead outside, but this northern horse would have better luck trying to scale the wall. One leg wouldn't fit through the holes in these bars. I search the walls of the alcove covering the back gate and see what I am after: a ring of iron keys hanging above the sleeping guard. I make my way up the wall, put my teeth on the cool rusting metal, and am just about to pull it down, but the northern horse has other plans. He rears up tall on his two back legs, and slams his hooves down hard on the gate, denting it, but also sending a clanging echo across the castle grounds.

"God's body!" the fat guard yells out, jumping to his feet but falling straight back down again. The horse rears up and brings his strong hooves down once more on the metal gate. The place where the metal meets stone cracks and sends gray rock flying like flour off a baker's hands. The fat guard lifts himself by pressing the base of his spear into the stone floor, and pushing against it to steady and straighten his knees. He tilts the spear toward the horse who is rearing up to kick down on the iron gate for a third time.

I jump from the wall onto the guard, aiming for the meat of his neck. My claws latch onto his flesh and the force of my landing sends him into a spin. His dropped spear hits the floor with a clang and I bite down. Hot blood fills my throat.

Hooves crash into the iron-gate and it explodes out of the stone awning, hitting the earth outside of the castle, bent and deformed metal thudding into damp dirt.

I feel fat fingers digging into me. Blood leaks through my fur. My insides constrict. I see the horse running down the sloping hill, away from the castle, into the forest. The guards on the wall yell into the night and blood drips over my eyes. Human hands break flesh and tighten inside me. I exhale.

****

The sound of crashing metal can be heard in the dungeons. The screaming too—yells that echo through the darkness. The boy, Terryn, the twelve year-old son of a black smith, has been living in months and months of darkness and hasn't eaten for a week. Nothing is real to him, and he barely stirs awake when he hears the turmoil above. He knows the noise will end as all hallucinations do and whispers will follow.

"There's war outside," a voice says. It could be the man in the cell next to Terryn or it could be his own mind. He doesn't know and barely cares.

"Per'aps we'll be freed," another voice supposes.

"Hush up or they'll come in and hang us," someone hisses, and the syllables echo down the hallway.

I wish they would hang us, thinks Terryn. *They have been promising to do that for months.* But they haven't hung him and for three months he has laid in the darkness listening to his mind bounce through the dungeons. Terryn sleeps without closing his eyes.

Light and more screams. Torches line the hallways, and for the first time in weeks, Terryn sees the bars that hold him in. Guards push a fat man to his knees in the hallway.

"How could you let him go, Rulf?"

"He was right in front of you!"

"The horse kicked up and knocked in the gate," Rulf explains desperately.

"The horse is strong," one of the guards agrees.

"The horse is gone is what he is. Rulf's working with those western barbarians!"

They all talk over each other, encircling Rulf, who's on his knees, bleeding from the neck.

"Oy!" the man in the cell across, wearing clothes of burlap, calls out, trying to get the attention of the five guards in their gleaming silver suits. They don't look up from the fat man. One guard pulls a dagger from his hip.

"Sorry, Rulf. King's orders."

The knife goes slowly into the eye of the fat man; his screams pour out of him slowly, too. The noise is like sap dripping down a tree, sticking in the hallway instead of bouncing off the walls.

"Oy!" the man in burlap yells again.

Blood splatters and stains the armor of the man with the knife. He forces the dagger into the other eye.

"You don't need 'em Rulf. All you do is sleep anyway."

"Oy!" The man in burlap is standing at the bars, shaking them, clanging the metal.

"Shut it!" The guard with the knife turns to the man and holds it out, pointing it at him. "Or I'll do your tongue next!"

"You said the 'orse is gone. Which 'orse?" the man in burlap asks. "The gray from the north?"

"Aye. Now shut it or die." The guard puts the knife right up against the man in burlap but the man doesn't flinch.

"I can 'elp. The king wants 'im back, yes? I can 'elp track 'im."

"I told you to shut up!" A guard grabs the man's rough clothes through the bars and lifts him off his feet.

Quick to intervene, another guard puts his arm onto the shoulder of his angry friend. "That's the stable master. And we need to find the horse or we'll all be swinging in nooses."

Only if you're lucky, thinks Terryn.

The angry guard drops the man in burlap to his knees.

"Aye, let me out. I'll bring 'im back." The stable master, on his knees, rubs the back of his neck. "None of us need 'ang if I bring the 'orse back, eh?"

"Open the cell."

Terryn watches the iron key slide into the cell door of the stable master. The stable master stands and walks out, free. After seeing that, the lie falls out of Terryn's mouth, "I can help him. I worked the stables."

The stable master looks Terryn over and clenches his jaw, looking around the cells to see if anyone else wants to try out this lie.

The guards ignore Terryn and drag the fat man, bleeding in a heap, across the wet floor, shoving him into the stable master's former cell.

Terryn speaks louder, louder than he's ever spoken to a man in silver armor. "He'll need help bringing back the horse, sirs. He's a large one, and unruly. I led all the horses 'round the stables, never had no problem. I can help, truly I can."

Everyone turns to look at Terryn now, the five guards and the stable master; even Rulf with the bleeding eyes is staring, waiting.

"Aye," the stable master says, eyes narrowing. "I know the boy; 'e looks small, but 'e can pull an 'orse as good as any."

The largest guard nods. "The more men looking the better." A key slips into the door of Terryn's cell. "Make sure you bring him back or we're all dead."

****

Terryn and the stable master chew on rotting fruit, garbage for the livestock that the guards threw at them before sending them out of the castle walls. In the open air, the colors of the rising sun stain the morning sky. Even this modest amount of light hurts their eyes, but the pain is welcomed. They pass the tree line and the dampness of the forest settles into their lungs. Branches hit Terryn's face and scratch his skinny arms.

Terryn and the stable master are tired and weak. They walk slowly, but so do the guards. The guards are scanning the trees for barbarians from the west. Soon, Terryn and the stable master are far ahead of the two guards sent to accompany them. The only indication that they aren't lost completely is the faint clanging of metal somewhere behind them.

"Well, you ain'ts a stable boy. We know that," the stable master says with a sneer. "You know anything at all 'bout 'orses?"

"No," Terryn says.

The stable master shakes his head and spits into the dirt.

"But I touched this one, the north horse. The king walked it through the city. I snuck up and pet the hair on its back. The horse was mad because—" Terryn looks back to make sure no one is listening and shifts his volume to a whisper. " —the guards were whipping it down the streets. I calmed it down by petting and singing to it. Then the king saw, threw me in the dungeon, and said he would hang me."

"Aye, I 'eard. Why ain'ts you 'anged then?"

"Don't know," Terryn says.

"Aye. I should 'ave been 'anged. Look 'ere," the stable master says, pointing to a bush with a streak of blood across it. "This 'orse bleeds when 'e runs. Sweats blood . . . or so the king tells us."

Terryn nods. "We follow the blood and we find the horse."

"You ain'ts dumb. That's good," the stable master says, pulling a leaf off the bush and sticking it in his mouth. They continue to follow the blood like that: scanning the tree line for any trace of red and stopping every so often for the stable master to taste whatever they find. Behind them, the sound of the armor clinks faintly in the trees.

Then the trail stops. There is no thread to follow, no blood for the stable master to taste. Terryn looks over every branch and leaf but cannot find any sign of the northern horse. When Terryn gives up looking, the guards barrel through the trees.

"Why are you stopped?" the larger guard asks.

Terryn starts to speak, but the stable master pinches the skin of his arm.

"Sun's going down. Can't track in the dark," the stable master says.

The guards accept this answer. The four bed down as the sun sets.

Terryn lies awake on the hard root-covered ground; months spent in the darkness have made this moonlight seem as bright as the sun. He sees every impression on every leaf as he stares up into the tree above him. Stars poke through the layers of branches. *My eyes shouldn't work this well*, Terryn thinks. *Perhaps I'm still in the dungeon and this is all fantasy.* The snores of the guards could be the snores of the men in the dungeons; the sound of the nearby river could be the water that leaks down the dungeon walls.

Terryn stands and relieves himself. Then, he walks through the brush and down an incline, heading to the river to quench his thirst.

That's where Terryn sees him—the horse, bathing in the river. It is just as the first time the king brought the animal through the city—the northern horse, the one who bleeds, the most beautiful creature Terryn has ever seen. Rows of muscles bulging from its back, its light gray skin is stained with a dark liquid—blood, the blood the stable master has been tasting all day. The river water sends the dark fluid downstream.

****

I see the boy on two legs. Remember him. I do not run as he wades into the water and reaches out for me. I breathe slowly so he knows I am unafraid. I listen as he whispers another song in my ear: a beautiful melody that lifts my heart, even if I cannot understand the words. He pulls his hand away and stares at his palm, wet with my blood. He's wondering if he should call out, call out to the guards, tell them he's found me, win his freedom, win the favor of the king along with it.

The boy kneels down and washes his hand off in the river, scrubbing it clean of blood, careful to get it out of every crack and impression on his palm. He points to the forest and nods, telling me to run.

I do not.

Instead, I kneel down for him. Can a creature with two legs understand?

The boy struggles to climb onto my back, holds the hair

of my mane too tightly—he's afraid, so I wait for his heart to settle, for his breathing to match mine.

Then, I run. I run with him on my back through trees and brush, through brambles and thorns, through dense forest and dark places, to the flat country, taking us both away from the camp, away from the castle, away from the king who locked so many of us in the darkness.

Inspiration
The One Who Bleeds is an original fairy tale based on the mythos surrounding a particular breed of horse called the Ferghana or Han Xue Ma, literally translated to mean a "sweats blood horse." These horses were rumored to be extremely fast and capable of maintaining high speeds for long distances and were greatly coveted by emperors during the Han Dynasty.

About the Author
Nick Vaky is a writer, filmmaker, podcaster, and recreational rabble-rouser. By day he works in video and film production, and by night he writes down stories of melting flesh, blood rituals, and slow descents into madness. Some of his work can be found on nickvaky.com, healthycriticism.net, and butternutdeluxe.com.

Heart/Clock

By Erisa Apantaku

Beth hates being woken up by her alarm. Snapped out of a dream by beep Beep BEEP! However, she adores waking up naturally. Slipping out of sleep like stepping out of a bath. Sometimes she lies in bed listening to the birds outside. Her neighbors readying themselves for the day. The clack of footsteps down the hallway of her apartment floor. The patter of rain on the pavement and cars outside.

Sometimes, she lies flat on her stomach on her largest, fluffiest pillow. And somehow, by some property of sound and cloth and air, she hears her heart beating. It isn't as crisp as listening with a stethoscope, but still. She can hear it. She can hear *me*—her heart—pounding in her chest, and it reminds Beth how amazing it is to be alive.

More recently, however, she has no time for this. Her coworker, Samuel, was fired and her boss, Jasper, has yet to find a replacement. Which means everyone—particularly Beth—has taken on a few extra duties.

A few, Beth. You're only supposed to have a few new

responsibilities.

Beth is the operations satisfaction specialist at Humanity Housing, a nonprofit organization dealing with housing inequality in the greater Hartford, Connecticut area. She is—in her words, not mine—a data monkey. "Spreadsheets all day, every day," she says to her friends when they ask her how work is going. Now, with Samuel gone, Beth has to take over grant writing and the liaison work with the outreach teams.

For the past several weeks, she has been sleeping less. As soon as her head hits the pillow, her mind races with thoughts of the day that was and the day that will be. Her mind floats from budget reports to housing loan forms. She worries she won't finish everything she needs to finish each week. She'll fall behind and people will go homeless. People are already homeless, she thinks. But MORE people will go homeless. And it will be her fault. And with winter approaching....

So she is sleeping less, and thus eating more. That's a thing. When you sleep less, you eat more. Trust me. After being in Beth for twenty-six years, I know the ins and outs of weight gain patterns, hormonal shifts, circadian rhythms, blah blah blah.... And less exercise. Beth's missed the past four weeks of yoga classes. This is a dangerous downward spiral.

****

One morning, Beth wakes up before her alarm, a shooting pain in her back.

Immediately, she thinks: *heart attack.*

The weeks of waking up stressed have finally done her in. Done *me* in, I suppose, and thus her.

That's what she *thinks*. But when she shifts a bit, she realizes she's fallen asleep on her alarm clock—a cheap, plastic, analog thing. I'm pumping just fine. So Beth takes the clock from her bed and places it back in its proper position on the nightstand.

****

On Monday of the seventh week of work hell, Beth wakes up, again, before her alarm. She doesn't roll over onto her stomach to listen for me. She doesn't even put her hand over her chest to feel me. Instead, she begins thinking of the mounting pile of work that has accumulated over the past six weeks and that tightness in her chest comes back. And it hooks her, pulls her out of bed, drags her to the shower, to a toast and butter breakfast, onto a bus ride, up a flight of stairs, into a break room with a lukewarm coffee cup in her hand, behind her desk with her eyes glued to her screen.

A day of this, an evening of microwaved leftover dinner, and then sleep.

I understand. Her heart's in the right place.

Metaphorically.

Beth doesn't want to slack on her job. She helps provide housing to underprivileged, marginalized populations. What can she do? Give up? A report on housing loans is due by five o'clock. Should she eat lunch when so many people are suffering and she has the power to do something about it? She's behind on updates to the legal department. She should stay late to catch up. Of course. She must.

****

On Tuesday, Beth wakes up before her alarm. She lies in bed thinking of all the things scheduled for that day like an athlete visualizing a race: a lunch meeting with the council, a report on anti-discrimination practices due on Linda's desk by the afternoon, replying to her growing list of emails. She rolls onto her stomach, onto her large, fluffy pillow, and tries to listen to me. Instead she hears the tick-tick-tick of her alarm clock. Has she left it in her bed again? She shifts her pillow, but the clock isn't underneath it.

Beth looks at the nightstand. No clock. Instead:

LUB-DUB

There on.

LUB-DUB

Nightstand.

LUB-DUB

I am.

LUB-DUB

Beth sees me pushing air at a normal seventy beats-per-minute and she closes her eyes. She thinks this is a part of her dream. She thinks she's seen wrong. She opens her eyes. I'm still there.

LUB-DUB

She pokes me.

LUB-DUB

She rubs her finger on my (her?) left atrium.

LUB-DUB

She's fascinated.

LUB-DUB

She's scared.

LUB-DUB

I'm moist. Wet with a thin layer of blood. I'm hot. 98.6 degrees Fahrenheit. But I'm cooling down.

LUB-DUB

She picks me up in her hands and feels me contracting and expanding. A forceful, violent motion. But Beth holds me like she would a baby.

LUB-DUB

BEEP-BEEP-BEE-

From within her chest, the alarm clock erupts. The sound's muffled by her flesh, but it's still audible. But for Beth, it's not just a sound. Beth *feels* the clock's vibration through her body.

BEEP-BEEP-BEEP

How to make it stop?

Beth takes in some deep breaths. Some meditative deep breathing. She must calm down, she thinks. In and out. In through the nose, out through the mouth. In through the nose, out through the mouth.

BEEP-BEEP-BEEP

BEEP-BEEP-BEEP

BEEP-BEEP-BEEP

Clearly this is not working for her. After a minute of beeping and breathing, Beth loses her attempt at focus and calm. She bangs her fist against her chest.

"FUCKING SHUT UP!" she shouts into the empty air of her apartment. Her fists beat:

BANG-BANG-BANG

BEEP-BEEP-BEEP

"SHUT"-BANG-"THE"-BANG-"FUCK"-BANG-"UP."

Then a sterile silence.

****

Obviously you—a normal human—carry your heart around with you everywhere, but it must be weird carrying your heart around with you in a resealable plastic bag. I mean, people talk about wearing their heart on their sleeve, but firstly, that's a horrible analogy. Why you humans have decided to make the heart the "emotional" organ in the body, I have no idea. I control nothing. I am tugged along from place to place in this meat sack. Told to pump faster or slower by nerves from the brain like the whip on a horse. Why would *I* be the one to make you fall in love? Why would *I* be the one to make you nervous?

Secondly, "heart on your sleeve" is not literal. Beth is *literally* carrying me around in a plastic bag in her purse. It must be weird.

I assume her first thought—besides "I must be crazy, I should go to a psychologist"—is to go to a clinic. Right now Beth is on the bus with me in her lap (in her purse). We are probably not en route to a psychologist. Maybe we are. I don't know. Beth has never seen a psychologist before so I don't know where she would go to see one.

Instead, Beth has probably formed the following plan based on the two possibilities:

1) She is crazy and this is a hallucination.

2) She is sane and her heart has been replaced by an alarm clock.

If number two is correct, a psychologist can't really help her at present. Sure there will be a lot of emotional trauma to unpack once I'm back in her chest, but if number two is true, Beth needs a surgeon, not a shrink.

OK, but I think Beth reasons that number two is probably impossible, leaving only option one. But she doesn't have a psychologist, so in order to see one, she needs to make an appointment.

It could take days to weeks to actually get a consultation. So Beth is on the bus riding to a free clinic, I presume. And at the clinic she'll show the doctor the heart. And if the doctor says: "This is just a clock in a plastic bag," she will say, calmly, rationally: "I think I need a psychologist because I'm seeing a heart there and I think there's a clock in my chest."

This is what I *think* we're going to do, but on the bus, Beth gets a call.

"Hello?"

"Hello, Beth." It's her boss, Jasper. "Where are you?"

"I called in sick an hour ago."

"The meeting, Beth. We have a lunch meeting with the council. We can't cancel."

"But, I have the... flu."

"Are you bleeding out of your orifices?"

"No, but...."

"Then I need you to come in. Take a taxi. I'll pay the fare."

Beth gets off the bus at the next stop and hails a cab.

Throughout the taxi ride, she must be thinking about what to do with me. Surely she can feel me getting colder. She must sense that's not good. Well, none of this is good, I suppose. But doesn't this present her with some sense of urgency? The feeling of me beating in the purse in her lap is unsettling, right? Like the vibrating pulse of a cellphone signaling a call you're about to miss.

But eventually she closes her eyes; the steady beat of my contracting fibers has, apparently, calmed her.

****

The meeting with the development council goes as many meetings go—mostly a waste of time, mostly could have been handled remotely via email—but several important things are agreed upon. I sit in the purse on the floor while they lunch on sandwiches and pasta salad from the deli down the street.

After the meeting, Jasper pulls Beth aside.

"That was excellent. Thank you for coming in even though you were feeling sick. I don't think anyone else could've handled that question about the new zoning statute so well."

Beth nods, heads for the door.

Jasper calls her back: "Where are you going?"

"I have the flu."

"Oh, that's right." Jasper looks at her with suspicious eyes. "I forgot, since you don't really look sick."

"DayQuil." And Beth's out the door before he can hurl anymore backhanded criticism her way.

****

How does one get a heart back into one's body?

This is the question of the afternoon for Beth. She should've headed to the clinic after leaving work, but for some reason she's sitting at her kitchen table. I'm there on the table in the plastic bag. With the way she's staring at me, I think she might grab a fork and knife from the drawer, slice me into pieces, and eat me. I guess then I'd be back inside her. But she doesn't do this. She just stares. Thinking. About me, I assume. But she's sitting there for hours. She can't be thinking about me this whole time. Maybe she's thinking about the meeting today that, in retrospect, did go very well. Or maybe about tomorrow. What will happen tomorrow, in her appointments with the contractors?

She sits at her kitchen table for hours, until it gets dark and she gets too tired and hungry and has to make a quick peanut butter and jelly sandwich for dinner. She turns off the lights while I pump steadily on the table.

After a while I hear a fly buzz around. My plastic bag is protecting me from the insect and keeping me moist and as warm as possible post-extraction from my body. But I would hardly call this comfortable. I'm not supposed to be on a plate. I'm supposed to be in a chest. What the fuck, Beth? Hours sitting at the kitchen table, but you didn't get up to do anything. What could you be thinking about for *HOURS*, Beth? They could've done the surgery to put me back in the time it took for you to just sit there staring.

****

On Wednesday, Beth wakes up with a start at the sound of her alarm clock.

BEEP-BEEP-BEEP

She looks to the bedside table and doesn't see it. She checks in the drawer. No clock. Suddenly, the previous day comes back to her, and she slaps her chest until the beeping subsides. She lies in bed as I lie on the kitchen table.

LUB-DUB

TICK-TICK-TICK

LUB-DUB

A vibration stirs her to motion: a text from Jasper: "How are you feeling today? Will you be in?"

She bolts up from the bed and begins getting ready for the day.

****

At work, Beth is, objectively, the most efficient I've ever seen her. What's the expression? Don't think; just do. It's like Beth isn't thinking. She just does everything that is put in front of her. Devours it like a cold drink on a hot day. She drafts proposals all morning. She replies to emails at lunch. She analyzes four data sets in the afternoon and revises her proposals by three-thirty. Beth completes all the things she had planned for the entire week. It is only Wednesday. So Beth decides to leave early.

This is good. This is very good. I'm in her purse as she's about to leave work. We're headed for the door. I see us walking through it. We will get on the bus going to the hospital. Then we'll talk to a doctor. The doctor's eyes will widen when Beth reveals me pumping in my plastic bag. They'll rush her into surgery. There I'll be, beating in those sterilized stainless steel dishes. And then they'll cut her open at the sternum and there, wrapped in sinew and blood vessels, that shitty, goddamn alarm clock. And the surgeons will cut it out and put me back in my place. And then they'll stitch Beth's chest back up. And Beth will wake up in the hospital bed, and put her hand on her chest. And she'll smile, knowing all is well.

And this is the path I know we're going to take, this long but necessary path back to normalcy. I can feel it. But for some reason, Beth diverges, taking a turn down a hallway, and suddenly we're in Jasper's office. Why? I begin beating faster.

"Hi, Jasper, do you have a second?"

"Sure, Beth, what's up?"

Beth sits down.

"I deserve a raise." There's no hint of timidity in her voice. Jasper is not expecting this. He tightens up.

Beth continues, direct and to the point: "I've been doing the work of two people for the past two months. Either hire another person and reduce my workload, or give me a raise."

"Beth, your work is great."

"I know."

"But I think the organization just doesn't have the funds to raise salaries right now. Anybody's, not just yours."

"Then this organization doesn't have the right to my labor."

Beth gets up from the chair. I'm amazed. I can't contain my excitement. I'm afraid I may rupture my plastic bag.

"Beth, wait." She sits back down. Jasper continues: "We're doing important work at H3C. If you leave, we'd be in a crunch."

"Then pay me what I'm worth. I'm doing mine and

Samuel's work right now. I ought to get at least a fifty-percent increase in my salary."

"That's impossible, Beth. We're all overworked here."

Beth gets up from the chair.

Jasper pleads: "Beth, it's literally not possible. We don't have the funds."

"Then tell me what *is* possible, Jasper." Exacting. Her words a scalpel blade on Jasper's flesh. He squirms.

"I don't know." He sighs. "I'd have to talk with accounting. And this would have to be approved by the board."

Beth's voice has been even up until this point. Her words flow coolly, not catching in her throat. This atypical composure remains as she delivers her ultimatum: "I have four more days of sick leave. I'm taking them until I hear back from you. Next week, if there's no raise, I'm not coming in. So consider this my notice."

And she leaves the room.

Back in the hallway, I'm pounding in my plastic baggy. She can't hear me, though. She's hearing her shoes triumphantly strike the hallway floor. Then the rain against the pavement and cars and her umbrella. I'm beating faster, uncertain of where we're going; her pace is steady and determined. Then I hear the sound of music, the din of human voices, and drink glasses clinking. We're in a bar. Beth orders a vodka cranberry. She's sipping it.

This makes sense. We have been victorious today: finishing all our work; leveraging that efficiency to demand higher pay. We're not going to work tomorrow, so why not drink? I assume Beth is relaxed. She's chatting with the bartender and joking with another group of women out for happy-hour drinks.

And just when I'm starting to relax too, just when my rhythm is returning to the regular seventy beats-per-minute and I'm starting to worry less—for now—about the whole I-should-be-in-a-chest-but-I'm-in-a-plastic-bag situation, Beth hears: "Beth?"

She turns and it's Samuel and my thumping commences again, unnoticeable due to the bass of the song playing over the stereo system.

"Samuel! How are you?" They hug. They catch up. Samuel has found another job: temp work, so not great, but he's happy he's not unemployed. They both agree it's such an amazing coincidence they've run into each other. Samuel invites Beth to join him and his friends.

"Beth," Samuel says. "This is Jane, Michael, Blanca, and Devon."

"Hi," Beth says while sitting down.

"Hi, Beth!" Samuel's friends chime in.

"Beth used to be my co-worker."

"At the housing NGO?" Blanca asks.

"Yeah, I don't know how she stays at it."

Beth sighs. "Trust me, after you left it's only gotten worse. I basically handed in my notice today."

"Really?" Samuel asks.

"Well, everyone there is overworked and I told Jasper, my boss, it's unsustainable. I can't keep being worked to the bone for the same pay I'm getting. It's not fair."

Samuel tips his beer bottle at Beth. "Wow. That's ballsy."

Beth clinks her glass with his bottle and they both take a drink.

I feel tight. Constricted. I can't pinpoint why. But Beth, she's... laughing. She's smiling. She's enjoying the company of these strangers. Beth is apparently so charming, Blanca invites her to join their weekend league ultimate Frisbee team. Beth accepts. They're talking about current events, making jokes about Devon's failed *Tinder* dates, and discussing Samuel's new job options. The Samuel that Beth had a crush on when they worked together. Her words would often get caught in her throat when she spoke to him. Which was EVERY DAY. But today she's relaxed. Possibly flirting. Definitely having fun.

A little too much. Beth has a few too many drinks and Samuel has to help her out of the bar and into a cab. The rain is still coming down, although more lightly than before. Samuel tries to hail a taxi.

"Hey, so," Samuel begins, "tonight you should just go home and sleep. But if you're free tomorrow... or Friday? Maybe we could get together?"

"I would *love* that," she says. They both smile. A taxi pulls up to the curb. "I'll call you tomorrow?"

"Sure."

Beth turns to enter the cab and trips on a cracked piece of sidewalk. Her bag falls to the ground. *I* fall to the ground. And I roll slightly out of the purse, my baggy feeling the wet, cold concrete and the drops of rain that fall against my plastic protection. And Samuel, being a good person, scoops up the purse and then goes to scoop me up. And his eyes illuminate with terror at a human heart in a plastic bag.

"What is this?"

He grabs me, and I beat faster, causing him to freak out

71

and drop me again against the pavement.

"Oh, shit," Beth lets out like a sigh.

"Beth, what the…. Is this…?" He looks at me closely. "Is this a heart?"

"Wait, you can see this?"

The cab beeps. From the front seat, the driver shouts: "Are you in or out?"

Beth picks me up, puts me in front of Samuel's face: "Can you see this heart?"

BEEP-BEEP

LUB-DUB

"YES! WHAT THE FUCK ARE YOU DOING WITH A HEART?"

"Thank GOD!"

Beth drops me back in her purse and slides into the cab. She slams the door and says: "DRIVE." Samuel stands shocked on the curb. His image shrinks in the rearview mirror as we drive away.

Thank GOD, I echo. She knows I'm real. She knows it's all real. I'm beating even faster now, not from fear but from joy. Now we can go to the hospital unafraid. We can go and get the surgery.

"Where are we going?" the taxi driver asks.

And she tells him our apartment.

****

Just like the night before, we sit at the kitchen table. Me on it, her in the chair beside. She stares at me as I beat. And I'm still beating fast. I'm anxious. I assume she's thinking about what to do with me. She knows I'm real. She can't deny this any longer. She should do something. She should get up and do something. We need to do something, Beth. This is not natural. I need to be inside a person. If not you, someone else. Donate me, Beth. You can donate me to someone who needs a heart.

But we just sit there. For an hour she doesn't get up to do anything. Because she doesn't care about me anymore? Because there is no tightness in her chest?

Then she gets up, turns off the lights, and goes to bed.

****

I'm cold, in the dark, on the plate, in the kitchen, after Beth has gone to bed. I'm thinking about where it all went wrong. Beth was letting her work stress her out, and as a result, she was stressing me out. Part of me hoped this whole situation would make her appreciate me more. This assumption was clearly wrong. I now think Beth does not care about me at all.

She doesn't need me. *I'm* the problem. As I said, Beth is objectively better without me. Her clock is even, steady. It's like she's in a perpetual state of meditation. Her clock does not tick faster for Jasper or Samuel or project proposals or meetings with the council. Her clock doesn't bend to the whip of her brain like I did. Her clock ticks sixty times every sixty seconds.

****

In the morning, Beth lies in bed. Her alarm clock has already woken her up and she's lying in bed, smiling to herself. I guess because she's satisfied with having the day off and with waiting to hear from Jasper about the raise. She's probably unconcerned about whether it will happen or not. She must also be unworried about what Samuel thinks of her and me. I think I should've stopped worrying about Beth a long time ago.

This morning Beth came to see me in the kitchen. She finally took me out of the plastic bag. I now sit in a clear, glass mason jar in Beth's bedside table drawer. The glass feels colder than the plastic, but I ought to get used to it. This will probably be my home forever, beside melatonin bottles, a dozen condoms, and a book Beth will never finish, has barely even started. I pump steady, seventy times every sixty seconds.

And I think: *why am I still beating?*

Inspiration

This is an original fairy tale I created specifically for the TWG Twisted Fairy Tales Anthology. The idea came at a time when I was very anxious and stressed and found myself wishing my heart would just chill. But stress is not something created by our hearts. Or our brains. Stress is something we allow to flow from the exterior world into our minds. The question is: What do you do about that?

About the Author

Erisa Apantaku creates things: stories, audiofiction, essays, film scripts. She regrets very few things in life, but one is that she'll never be able to see her bones, muscles, and other internal organs. This is her second story for a TWG Anthology, the first being "Algae" in *Peak Heat*. Her work often revolves around themes of identity, ecology, and movement. You can find more of her work at apeandtaco.wordpress.com.

Justify My Love

By C.K. Hugo Chung

The mediation by the serpent was necessary.
Evil can seduce man, but cannot become man.
--Franz Kafka

NYPD 5th Precinct
Thursday, June 9, at 10:30PM

"Thanks for coming in, Mr. McCarthy."

Detective Larry Sea poured himself and his client some neat whisky, and pushed it across the desk. Joe McCarthy, his client, took a courtesy sip, and put down the glass cautiously.

It was late at night on a weekday, but the precinct office, located in downtown Manhattan, was still bustling. A motley crew of misfits, mostly drunk or high, were reined in by the policemen. Occasional bursts of fury and hysteria shot through the drably lit place. Each interrogation desk formed its silo of varied human conditions, filled with palpable angst and malleable storylines.

Gazing out the window of Larry's office, Joe felt like he was about to be thrown overboard and drowned in the tempest in this teapot.

"What can I do for you, Detective?"

Larry lit his cigarette, took a deep drag. "A kid named Barry Wong," he said, and puffed out the smoke at Joe, a nonsmoker, causing him to feel a bit nauseous. "Do you know him?"

"No."

"His parents own a small noodle shop on Grant Street. Amazing wonton soup over there. Best comfort food after a whole night of bullshit." Larry blew the smoke at Joe's face again, and pointed his cigarette at the gothic scenes on the other side of the window.

Joe couldn't help but wave away the pungent fumes, getting more agitated.

"I've been going there for almost ten years, ever since I was transferred to this shitty precinct. The Wongs are nice to me, you know? They always give me a little extra: noodles, wontons, roast pork, and so on."

Though feeling testy, Joe didn't want to interfere with Larry's rambling; he was quite aware that he was here for a reason. He just didn't know why.

"This kid Barry, I first met him when he was ten. Already helped out in the shop. So scrawny with long arms. Hate to say it," Larry poured himself another drink and chugged it instantly, "but he looked like a monkey. A pet one, nonetheless."

Joe fidgeted a little bit. He crossed his legs to adjust. He could sense Larry's alcohol-infused soliloquy was about to get heavy. He wondered whether this was a confession or an interrogation.

"Anyway, one time I was so wasted, after celebrating a major bust of a prostitution ring. And…and…haha… I stumbled into the noodle shop, puked all over their table, which was a line I shouldn't have crossed with Mr. and Mrs. Wong. They were so furious; they cursed me out in Cantonese. Anyway…I was too washed out to explain or even clean myself up…but Barry, so sweet and understanding for his age, cleaned up my mess, and offered me a bowl of hot wonton soup, free of charge and the best in town."

Larry's voice trembled. He poured another drink for himself, and pulled out another cigarette.

"I love that kid. After all these years. He had it rough," Larry lit his cigarette, "and he worked hard. Always looked out for his family. Over the years he'd seek my advice: how to deal with local gangsters, or racist patrons…that sort of stuff. I felt like his mentor, even though he didn't dare to ask me. I wanted to protect him, you know?" Larry's gaze zoomed in on Joe's face, causing Joe to nervously swallow. "That's why when he disappeared a few weeks ago, I had to step in and find out what happened."

He aggressively blew out another line of smoke into Joe's face. This time Joe couldn't contain his annoyance.

"Please, Detective Sea, what's that got to do with me? I have no clue. Also, can you stop blowing smoke at me?"

"It has to do with your wife." Larry smirked.

"Blanche? What are you trying to say?" Joe was getting worked up. Larry's insinuation about his wife was beyond his comprehension. "What does she have to do with this Barry kid?"

Larry gulped down his drink and put out the cigarette. The air between them became so thick that Joe started to feel stifled.

"After Barry disappeared, I checked the street surveillance cameras thoroughly. Every single corner in this area. On the evening of May nineteenth, he was last seen in front of your store. He went in around 7:30PM."

"So what? A lot of street kids like him come into our store."

"Barry never came out from the store. Nowhere to be seen since then, as if he fell off the face of the earth."

"Are you sure?"

"Barry would never do anything like that to his parents. Mr. and Mrs. Wong are devastated and they don't know what to do," Larry said and lit another cigarette. Joe felt some sweat forming on his forehead, and worried that he would have to put up with another round of a stink attack.

"Did Blanche close the store that night?" Larry continued.

"I don't know. Maybe." Joe tried to sound as calm as possible. Larry was not wrong; Blanche was there. She always closed the store. "Did you talk to Blanche?"

"My colleagues did. She said nothing. They moved on."

Larry's tone dropped severely, which made Joe feel as if he were under a low sky before the breakout of a violent storm.

"Officially I wasn't assigned to this case," Larry went on, "so I can't do anything during the investigation. But I know something's wrong. I've been in this business long enough to sniff out the right corner."

"What do you mean? I don't have to answer any of your inquiries." Joe folded his arms and turned his face to the side.

Larry refilled his drink, chugged it, and thumped down the glass.

"Mr. McCarthy, if you don't work with me and find out about your wife's involvement with Barry's disappearance," he belligerently blew the smoke at Joe one more time, "I can guarantee that there will be nonstop harassment at your pharmacy. You will report back to this office so frequently that you won't have any time for your family. You are about to become a father, aren't you?"

Larry scoffed, and his eyes burned with vengeance.

Joe was stunned. He dropped his head and sighed.

"What do you want me to do?"

The master bedroom of the McCarthys
Friday, June 10, at 12:30AM

"Where have you been?"

When Joe walked into their bedroom, Blanche was brushing her hair by the dresser. She was clothed in a white satin nightgown that smoothly outlined her body, curved elegantly in the final weeks of pregnancy.

It was near midnight and her husband was soaked with alcohol. Joe was not a regular drunk, Blanche thought. "I can smell your liquor. What happened? Something wrong with the store today?"

"I was summoned to the police station earlier." Joe

mumbled as he unbuttoned his shirt, stripped off his pants, and immediately got into bed.

"Why is that?" Blanche put down her brush and turned around to face her husband, who sat up by the headboard, his man boobs slightly drooping.

Joe stared at her from a distance. "Do you know this kid Barry Wong?"

"Who?"

"Barry Wong, a Chinese kid who came into our store a few weeks ago."

"Did he? I wasn't aware."

"He was last seen in our store, near closing, and you were there, weren't you?"

"Is that so?" Blanche furrowed her brow and folded her arms.

"Come on, Blanche, I know you were there. Tell me what happened."

"What did the police tell you?"

"Not much. He wanted to find out what happened that night."

"Nothing happened. I'm not even sure who that person is." Blanche wouldn't budge.

"You gotta be kidding me! There's a person missing after visiting our store. Don't tell me you know nothing!" Joe raised his voice, sounding exasperated.

"Please...." In front of her husband, Blanche started to tremble, and her tears began to well up. "Joe, you have to believe me, because I really don't know anything. I've never seen this kid," she pleaded, sounding desperate.

"If that's the case, why was I questioned? Should I ask Esmeralda? Will she know about it?"

"No." Blanche dropped her voice straight away, startling Joe a little bit. She then switched it to her normal soft tone: "She wasn't even there. So let's not expand this seemingly ludicrous Barry-gate."

They both chuckled.

"Seriously, what should I do?" Joe gave in.

"Who is this officer?"

"Detective Larry Sea."

"Larry and Barry…huh…sounds like a comedy duo. You know what, I can take care of it."

Blanche turned around to finish brushing her hair. Both of them fell silent, deep in their thoughts.

"Trust me. I will make sure everything will be all right. Babe, you look so stressed."

Blanche's voice became tender. She slowly walked up to her husband, exuding her maternal pheromones. Joe laid his head on her belly to feel the subtle and miraculous pace of his baby's ever-moving position.

"You deserve a good night's sleep, my love." Blanche gave him a kiss and turned off the light.

Outside their bedroom, Esmeralda Snake, Blanche's younger sister, had been eavesdropping on their conversation with a dark expression.

Tiptoeing back to her room, Esmeralda pondered whether she should turn herself in to end the infliction on her family. It had already caused a disturbance and potential plight. She would need to do something to protect them.

The McCarthys' pharmacy
Thursday, June 16, at 10:30AM

"Don't be absurd, Ezzy. We can't let this crooked detective get the upper hand on us."

In the store's back office, Blanche was surprised to learn about Esmeralda's plan to voluntarily turn herself in to the police. "You changed the indoor security camera and destroyed the tape from that evening, didn't you?"

"Mm…yes," Esmeralda answered in a restless manner, and started to bite her nails.

"Are you sure? Did you follow my instructions to burn it in the back alley and replace it with some later recorded footage?" Blanche walked up to her sister, and stared into her eyes. "Listen. Everything will be fine. Let me talk to that rat detective first. I'll see him later this afternoon."

Blanche peeled Esmeralda's fidgeting fingers away from her mouth and wrapped them tightly in her hands.

****

Growing up together in the same adopted family, the Snakes, Blanche and Esmeralda, despite not being blood relations, were always close, as if they were real sisters.

Blanche remembered the day she turned ten. Her adopted mom, a flighty Snake, handed her a blanket-wrapped gift. She looked into the blanket, and there was an angelic-looking baby.

A shock, like an electric wave, sped through her little body. She wanted to scream, but she didn't want to disturb the sound sleep of the little treasure. With bated breath,

Blanche smiled and held it close to her chest.

"You seem to like this baby." The flighty woman lit her cigarette and continued, "So it is your responsibility now." She blew the smoke at Blanche's pure, ecstatic face.

Blanche felt that something solid had finally happened, especially in the abused and neglected chaos that was her life. This baby was hers.

NYPD 5th Precinct, same day, at 2:30PM

"Mrs. McCarthy, glad you could make the trip."

"Of course."

Blanche sat down across the desk from Larry. He couldn't help but admire this woman's natural beauty and grace, even at such a late stage of pregnancy. For a split second, he couldn't believe this warm, maternal human being could also be an icy, brutal suspect.

"What can I do for you, Detective Sea? I understand that you've spoken with my husband," Blanche stated solemnly.

"So you do know Barry Wong?"

"I can't say I remember him in great detail."

"He disappeared after visiting your store. Do you know anything about it?"

"Not really. He stopped by the store, browsed for a while, and he left."

"Really?" Larry leaned forward, staring directly into Blanche's eyes. "We don't have any record of him leaving the store."

"I don't own street cameras, so I wouldn't know what happened after he stepped out."

"Mrs. McCarthy, who else was in the store that evening?"

"No one but me."

"Is that so? Because my camera also showed that your sister, Esmeralda, rushed out of the store before you shut it down." Larry's tone firmed up, but Blanche's face didn't move a muscle. She began to smile instead.

"Well, there must be some confusion. Esmeralda was indeed in the store earlier that day. But I don't recall she and this kid coming across each other. Are you sure of the time when she left the store?"

Larry couldn't believe what he was hearing. This woman was flat-out lying. Shaking his head while sighing, Larry pulled out a cigarette.

"We are quite sure, Mrs. McCarthy." Larry stood up to look down on her, "and you shouldn't lie to law enforcement. Big trouble. So let me ask you one more time. Are you involved with Barry Wong's disappearance?"

"No." Blanche, still in her seat, looked up in a piercingly cold manner.

"OK, well, if you say so," Larry said, sitting back and taking a deep drag of his cigarette, "then I have no choice but to summon your sister Esmeralda for cross-examining. Speaking of her...I did a little digging prior to our meeting. She seems to have a *colorful* past, am I right?"

Blanche's expression finally changed. She paled. Pressing down his "gotcha leer," Larry briskly continued, "Why don't you tell me more about this sister of yours? What should I call her? Esmeralda, or...Edward?"

"She has nothing to do with this case," Blanche replied curtly.

"We shall see. I just find it quite interesting that Barry seemed to be aware of her 'condition' since they got to know each other two years ago."

He puffed out the smoke at Blanche, and she turned her face aside.

The apartment of the McCarthys, same evening, at 6:30PM

The moment Blanche got back to her apartment, she couldn't help but rush to the toilet bowl and throw up. Larry's suspicion about Esmeralda's involvement left her sick and feeling helpless.

Kicking off her heels and unbuttoning her blouse, Blanche laid down on the floor and rubbed her belly softly. Her tears began to trickle down her cheeks.

****

Blanche couldn't remember the exact first time she had been hit by her father, an overbearing daddy Snake. Like a deer in headlights, Blanche had never thought she could be protected, especially in this sleepy part of New York.

One summer afternoon when she was changing the diaper for the baby, the daddy Snake stormed in drunk, and started to squeeze her butt from behind. When his fingers slithered to her front, she could feel they were disgustingly moist, his breath threateningly putrid.

Terrified, Blanche writhed out of his touch, grabbed the baby, and ran outside.

Hyperventilating while running, with nowhere to go,

Blanche felt like she was losing her mind until she and the baby crashed into some boy from the neighborhood.

"Woah...watch out! Are you all right?"

He stumbled back a few steps, steadied himself, and took a gander at this panic-stricken girl, who was holding a wailing baby and couldn't stop quivering.

"Can I help you?"

Blanche didn't answer; she looked back at him with a hollow gaze.

"I'd like to help you. But I don't know how. Is there anything I can do?"

Smiling shyly, the boy comforted her as if she were wrapped in a cashmere blanket, like the baby in her arms. Color gradually came back to her face.

Blanche began to cry; those tears first felt like drizzle, then they became a deluge.

"OK.OK...tell me what happened?" he asked.

Shaking her head frantically, she finally uttered a few blurry words: "He...he...he is a mon...monster...."

"Who is he?"

"My father...he's always so angry...and he likes to throw things after drinking...I don't mind the bruises, but this time, he...his fingers...he put them...I tried to push them away...but they kept...."

Blanche couldn't spit out any more words. A ten-year-old had no vocabulary for this kind of horror.

"What an asshole!" The boy was stunned by her confession, and started to get riled up. "We have to do something. Just stay here. I'm going to find us some help."

He looked her in the eyes and gripped her tightly around her arms as assurance. "Don't move. I'll be right back! I promise!" He skittered away backwards, shouting loudly, before turning around to sprint ahead at full speed.

Blanche didn't know how long she stood there. Completely blank. The baby finally stopped crying and fell back to sleep. All of a sudden, her twirling world came to a stop. She could hear birds softly chirping from a distance, and her baby's tender breath undulated harmoniously with hers.

"Hey! We're back!"

The boy returned with a squad of teenagers, all testosterone-fueled; they went back together to her house, trashed the living room, dragged the wasted daddy Snake to the basement, stripped him naked after tying him up on a chair, and started pissing all over his body while he was kicking and screaming.

"Come to my house. You are not safe here. Maybe you and the baby can stay with us for a while. Mom and Dad won't mind." He said it as gently as ever; meanwhile, the other boys were ransacking the remaining beverages in her house.

She nodded, held the sleeping baby closely to her heart. When they walked out, Blanche followed the boy.

"I'm Blanche. What's your name?" she asked, timidly.

The boy turned around, smiling, sunny and fresh as the first day on a beach.

"Joe. Joe McCarthy."

The living room of the McCarthys, same evening, at 8:30PM

In the living room, Esmeralda and Joe were furious after listening to Blanche's recounting of her interview with Larry Sea. Esmeralda even dropped a teacup on the ground, breaking the porcelain.

"Calm down, Ezzy, we need to figure out the way to fight back." Blanche, in her white robe, sounded exhausted.

"But what can we do?"

Feeling clueless and helpless, Joe put his face in his hands.

"Maybe we can negotiate with him." Blanche was talking to herself, hoping to come up with an idea.

"Why do we need to negotiate? If this Barry kid didn't vanish from our store, why do we care? Even though what he said about Esmeralda's past was…tasteless." Joe looked up from his palms, only to be met with guilty gazes from the Snake sisters.

"Well…there's something I need to confess." Standing by the fireplace, Esmeralda was murmuring to the cave, looking darker than ever.

"What? Esmeralda, what are you trying to tell us?" Joe turned to Blanche to search for some clues, but she just looked away and sighed.

"What's going on here? What am I missing?" Joe was on the verge of hysteria. He clasped his fists so tight that the veins underneath were ready to burst.

"We *killed* Barry Wong."

Esmeralda turned around to face Joe, who was shell-shocked. Blanche shook her head forlornly.

"Yo, Ezzy, not happy to see me?"

When Barry swaggered into the store, dressed in those silly balloon pants, she burst out laughing.

Even though they were the same age of nineteen, Esmeralda always felt that Barry had acted the same way since they'd first met. She'd just turned seventeen when starting to work in the store; then, he was a try-hard gangster messenger for the landlord. Full of lame swag that didn't fit. Two years later, he hadn't changed a bit.

"What ya want?"

Leaning against the counter, Esmeralda went back to flipping through a magazine, nonchalantly.

"Gotta collect my due here. It's time. You know the drill."

Barry jumped and sat on the counter, his ass landing on her page. She stepped back, arms folded, and stared at him with great annoyance.

"This is a low month, and you know we haven't stocked up enough inventory. Why can't you cut us some slack? Come back next month? I guarantee you will be paid double." Esmeralda sighed, trying to reason with him.

"Can't. Big boss won't wait. Ya know the Italians. They own us! Besides, I'm also on a tab—ya know my parents' noodle shop. They are behind on the rent. Mafia don't budge, and there's a goddamn deadline. I gotta help them."

Barry jumped down to the ground with a thump.

"Listen. We're all victims here. Can't we figure out a way to deal with this?"

Switching her strategy, Esmeralda stepped forward, leaned her upper body to the side of the counter and showed her deep cleavage. "I mean, we had some fun before. Can't that extend our probation period?" She put on a mischievous grin.

"Mamacita, this ain't gonna work. Give me the cash or some merchs to sell so that we can all live in peace."

"Ugh…that's impossible. Blanche won't agree." Esmeralda swung back from the counter, palms up as if she'd run out of treats. "Come on…Barry…let's talk in the back office?"

She reached out to touch Barry's hand. As had happened before, she could always find a way to persuade this awkward boy into extending their security fee, normal for this neighborhood.

"Yo, back off, you she-male freak! Not today!"

Barry slapped her hand away, strode to the aisle, and pushed down one of the shelves.

"What are you calling my sister? What is going on here?"

Blanche walked into the store, only to find her sister being disrespected by a clownishly clad kid. She stood in front of him, both hands on her waist.

"Blanche, that's OK. It's between me and Barry. Let me handle this." Behind Barry's back, Esmeralda pleaded.

"Step back, preggo lady, I'm gonna take what I need to lay off your asses." Barry strut over to another shelf stacked with over-the-counter drugs and started to raid it. "I don't give a damn about you or your freak sis. All I need is my cut."

Blanche stepped forward to death grip his wrist. "Stop what you're doing. We are in the red this month and can't afford your nonsense!"

"Get off or I'll cut you, bitch!" Barry forcefully slapped out of Blanche's grip, making her wobble a little.

"Don't you ever lay your hand on my sister!" Esmeralda pulled out a gun and pointed it at Barry, firming up her threat.

"Just leave for now. You are welcome to come back next month when we have the money ready." Blanche tried to negotiate, but her open fury quickly morphed into a haughty smirk at Barry, who felt like a schmuck in the ridiculous standoff.

"Don't be so condescending. I've had enough of that from you people in my life. You won't stop me!"

Barry moved up and pushed Blanche aside. She hit another shelf. He switched to another aisle, ruthlessly bagging all of the medicine.

Suddenly, there was a bang. Linear, loud, with trailing smoke.

Barry felt something, so fast and solid, that pierced through his skull and came out of his forehead.

He knelt down and fell forward.

"Oh my god! What have you done?" Blanche screamed and looked back at her sister in disbelief. Esmeralda went blank. She bit her nails, swayed back and forth, and dropped the .45 revolver to the ground.

Pier 25, same night, at 10:30PM

"Snap out of it!"

Blanche slapped the zombie out of a zonked-out Esmeralda. The Snake sisters stood by the Hudson River bank and waited for the body bag to sink down little by little.

It was a full moon, and its light accentuated the shadow on their faces.

Anxious and frightened, Esmeralda bit her nails and said fearfully, "What will happen to us?"

"It's gonna take the police a while to connect the dots." Blanche's voice became quite distant. "But I'll take care of it. I promise you."

Esmeralda turned around to face Blanche. She put her head on her big sister's shoulder.

"We are family."

Blanche touched her sister's fallen face tenderly, and kissed her on the forehead.

The McCarthys' Pharmacy
Thursday, June 30, at 10:30AM

Standing in front of the store's sign, with its snow-white background and blood-red cursive fonts that read *McCarthy's, Since 1976*, Larry Sea lit up a cigarette and blew out circles of smoke at it.

It had been a month and a half since Barry had disappeared. The investigation was bottlenecked at this point due to insufficient intelligence. Larry was mad because he wasn't in charge, even though he had called in

Joe and Blanche for the unauthorized interviews.

"You need to let go of the McCarthys, Sea, coz there's nothing. Don't go behind our back and screw up the case!" the assigned officers yelled at Larry.

Those incompetent colleagues and their futile attempt, Larry thought, by looking at the wrong places. He knew he could find something if he was there in the store. He could no longer contain his anger over the fact that the McCarthys still stayed at large while the Wongs were falling apart.

After rubbing off the cigarette butt under his shoe, Larry strode into the pharmacy. Esmeralda was behind the counter, browsing some gossip magazine.

"Miss Esmeralda Snake?"

Looking up, she answered casually. "Can I help you?"

"Detective Larry Sea from the precinct. Do you know Barry Wong?"

"Not really."

"He came here last month, didn't he?" Larry tried to sound as calm as possible; sweat beads were forming on his upper lip.

"Maybe. I don't quite remember." Esmeralda briskly shrugged off his questioning, which annoyed Larry immediately.

"Don't try to fool me, young lady; I know you'd been friends for a long time. He used to come here every month. I also happen to know he and you were intimate, despite...how should I say it...the 'transitioning'...."

"Listen, Detective, I know what you're after. My sister and I didn't do anything wrong. This kid was a crook and a gangster, and he tried to blackmail us for his personal gain. I urge you to—"

"HOW DARE YOU SPEAK ABOUT HIM LIKE THAT!"

Larry pounded down his fist on the counter in full-throttle rage. Esmeralda stepped back, shocked and frightened. Blanche and Joe rushed out from the back office.

"What the hell is going on?" Joe yelled at Larry and stood in front of both women.

"Mr. McCarthy. I must ask you to step aside. I need to take those two ladies back for the investigation." Larry said this vindictively while brushing against the gun holster strapped at one side of his hip. Everyone froze.

"Detective, you have no search warrant, nor the authorization for any arrest on my property, so I know you are bluffing," Joe replied firmly.

"I know it's one of you, or both of you, who are responsible. I won't leave until I have this cold-blooded scum in my hand!" After his fear-mongering cover was blown, Larry manically scowled at the McCarthys.

Blanche stepped up by her husband and held his hand tightly.

"But if you'd like," Joe cleared his voice a little bit, "I can go back with you to the station. Please leave them alone."

"Joe! What are you doing?" Blanche turned to her husband in disbelief.

"Then come with me, Mr. McCarthy." Larry pulled out two fingers to gesture Joe to move away from behind the counter.

"I will be fine. Don't you two worry about it." After hugging his family tightly, Joe walked out with his head high.

"These witches…." Larry murmured as he stepped out.

Blanche and Esmeralda stood there watching Joe follow Larry out of the pharmacy. Both of them felt this could be the last time they saw him, as if he were drowning in quicksand. Esmeralda started to tremble as Blanche silently cried.

****

Blanche never forgot that day, the first time of feeling protected, even after she and baby Edward were forced to return to the danger zone that was their broken home.

It would take Blanche another decade to escape fully from the Snakes. But eventually she moved out of the house for college, despite the fact that Edward had started to show all kinds of signs as a troubled child. Simply put, he hated his body. Everything was there from the get-go: his tendency to steal their mother's clothes and make-up, his being beat up by the kids from school, and most hurtful of all, his multiple attempts of suicide.

At first she didn't know what to do. She had to run again, this time alone.

Years later Blanche finally managed to take Edward in when he turned seventeen, the age of consent in New York. They cramped together in a tiny studio apartment in downtown. Their bathtub was in the kitchen. But she was happy to reunite with her baby brother, and beginning to dream about a family of her own.

Leveraging her physical beauty like a bejeweled serpentine belt, Blanche went into social climbing for survival. She received glamorous gifts and decent amounts of cash to support her family. But the material comfort never derailed her search for her first love, the boy who'd pissed on the monster for her when she was ten.

One time at a fundraising dinner for the Wildlife Conservation Society, Blanche was the arm candy of an uptown dandy for the evening. When she saw Joe, she couldn't believe after all those years his smile could still warm her heart. She walked up to him. At first he didn't recognize her. But it didn't really matter. She would never let him slip away, the most outstanding piece to complete the puzzle of her safety net.

NYPD 5th Precinct
Friday, July 1, at 4:30PM

"I am here for the bond of Mr. Joe McCarthy."

The next day, Blanche showed up at the precinct with a stack of bills to bail out her husband.

Even though there were still a couple of weeks before the estimated delivery time, she felt the kid in her belly was getting anxious. Rubbing her belly under a white linen dress, she gingerly whispered—

"This is not the right time, baby. Mommy's gotta get Daddy out first."

The police didn't take her money. Feeling a little confused, Blanche was led to see Larry, who looked smugly calm behind his desk.

He had a glass of whiskey in front of him and the smell of alcohol made her feel a bit nauseous. She didn't want to sit down. One hand on top of her belly and another around her waist, she tried to finish what she had to say as soon as possible.

"I killed Barry Wong," Blanche stated in a defeated manner. "What should I do to make an official confession?"

Larry didn't respond right away; instead, he just took a sip of that whiskey.

"You don't have to do it. Esmeralda already turned in the store's surveillance tape earlier today. We have her in our custody for an interview. Joe is ready to be released. You are more than welcome to meet him at the front desk."

"What...?" Blanche couldn't believe what she'd just heard. Her face was turning pale. Esmeralda had promised her that she would destroy the tape. "When did she come in?"

"Earlier this afternoon, I think. She was by herself."

The McCarthys' Pharmacy, earlier that day, at 12:30PM

"See you later. Have a good one."

When Blanche was in a hurry leaving the store to go to the bank (they'd had to fire-sell some inventory to come up with the amount needed for the bail), Esmeralda, behind the counter, was waving her a formal goodbye that felt unusual to Blanche.

"Well...OK...is everything all right?" Blanche turned around before stepping out of the store, asking with a bit of concern.

"Don't worry. I can take care of myself."

Esmeralda sounded relaxed and grinned widely. In spite of the store's dull light, Blanche thought that her sister, momentarily, was shining like an emerald gemstone.

NYPD 5th Precinct, later that afternoon, at 4:45PM

"Can...can I see her?"

Blanche's voice was quivering.

"Well, I have to see if they've finished the interview. But we spoke before she was taken in. Esmeralda took the full responsibility of pulling the trigger, and sinking Barry's body down in the Hudson River."

Larry was about to pull out a cigarette, but after glancing at a distressed Blanche, he paused and changed to pouring more whiskey into his glass.

"Esmeralda...she...she didn't know what she was doing. She was trying to save me from being hurt....It's all me...me...you know...?"

Feeling dizzy, Blanche grabbed the back of the guest chair tightly to steady herself.

"Are you all right? Do you need to sit down?" Larry stood up.

Suddenly, both of them heard a splash. Blanche looked down. Her maternal flood might not keep her family intact, after all.

"Geez, the water...I...I'll call an ambulance for you,

hold on...." Larry picked up his phone and asked fervently for help. Blanche, soaking wet, finally took a seat. Larry was calling and yelling, followed by multiple people running around. Joe rushed to her side and held her hands, and everything else began to peter out in her ears.

In her hazy vision, Blanche saw a figure in the distance. She couldn't be sure of who it was. But she felt she knew.

Bathed in a hopeful spring, she closed her eyes.

****

On his eighteenth birthday, Edward finally revealed his true identity to Blanche. She knew the day would come. He begged for her understanding, and the help, desperately—

"I can't live like this anymore! I'm dying! Can't you see? I am not supposed to be the person in this body!"

Biting his nails so hard they bled, Edward had the ultimate meltdown, and Blanche hugged him steadfastly.

"Tell me again, if you were a girl, what name would you pick?" Blanche whispered to Edward when they were in the hospital, ready for the operation.

"Oh...Blanche, I've told you so many times...."

Under anesthesia, Edward's voice drew out slowly.

"But I want to hear it one more time," Blanche implored, blinking her teary eyes.

"OK.OK...I've picked Esmeralda. Always liked that name. That's how I feel about my change. The new me, my new life, will sparkle like an emerald!"

Esmeralda grinned widely. She was shining.

Downtown Hospital, same evening, at 6:30PM

Lying in bed, Blanche could feel Joe's hand solidly in hers, and the feeling of protection was crawling back. It wasn't there yet, she thought to herself, but it was coming.

The puzzle, once again, was almost finished.

Not running away this time, Blanche swore to herself that she would do everything to bring her sister back. Her family wouldn't be broken up. Her love was strong. She was not afraid anymore.

A happy ending was in the making, for the Snake sisters, and their future.

Inspiration

This story is a noir twisting of *The Legend of White Snake* (白蛇傳), combined with '70s and '80s cult classics. The legend, nearly 1,000 years old, is one of the most famous stories in Chinese folklore.

About the Author

CK Hugo Chung is Taiwanese by nature, New Yorker by nurture. Writing in both Chinese and English, his essays, poetry and short stories can be found in various bilingual publications. He is the co-founder of a NYC-based writers' collective, Writeous, and Taipei-based artist studio, ColorWolfStudio.

His first book, *Writeous Accents*, will be released in early 2017. He is a proud member of Taipei Writers Group. For more information, please visit: https://www.facebook.com/Writeous2008

Instagram: @ckhugowriteous
Twitter: @Writeous1

Whispers

By Whitney Zahar

"Say: I seek refuge with the Lord and Cherisher of Mankind,
...From the mischief of the Whisperer (of Evil), who withdraws
(after his whisper)-
(The same) who whispers into the hearts of Mankind-
Among Jinn and among men."
--Quran, sura 114 (Al-Nas), ayat 1-6, a description of the
Shaytan

We came from nothing, created from smokeless fire. We are just as inclined towards good as evil. Most of my kind, the Shaytan, prefer to whisper into man's hearts and lead them as we see fit.

Just like man, my kind was created through free will. Who is to really say that the whispers in one's heart are not truly their own?

Who is to say what is really evil, if it leads one to the right place?

****

I was off-duty, standing in front of a small mosque, headscarf trailing between my fingertips in an almost-tangible reminder of who I was, where I was, and what I was about to do. I dragged my hand through my hair, glanced back over my shoulder, always alert like the good soldier I am. When I looked back at the mosque, I saw a little man in the doorway. He didn't see me, or he pretended not to; I'm not sure which. His head bowed over his clasped hands, in time with the vibrating chants praising Allah's name.

I approached the doorway of the mosque, but I could go no further. It was dark and cool inside, and for some reason, even this contrast to the heat of the dusty city didn't set me at ease. The surge of tension blazed through my being as much as the low drone of prayers in the dark space.

I stumbled backwards, away from the mosque, dazed and hollow. I tripped over the shawl I had tied around my legs to show modesty when I entered the mosque. When I reached the motorcycle that I had stashed down a side street, I ripped off the shawl in a daze. I fumbled with my keys, barely taking a moment to breathe or collect myself.

I had my eyes closed when I twisted the key.

The engine clicked a little before revving up. Then, all was silent.

Time stopped. The air sucked in, and released with force and heat.

I had my eyes closed when I entered hell.

No one expected me to live. My injuries were terrible. My skin had been torn and melted by burning shrapnel, especially my legs. My scalp was crisscrossed with lines of crimson, black, and blue, a jigsaw puzzle shattered and put together again with many stitches.

Broken leg, shattered collarbone, cracked ribs. IEDs can break a person in many ways. Improvised Explosive Devices. Easy to make. Easy to hide. Easy to devastate.

But the worst injury of all was that I lost my head. Literally. After I regained consciousness, the doctors told me that it was called atlanto-occipital dislocation, an internal decapitation. When I was thrown from my motorcycle during the explosion, my head struck the ground so hard that I did more than crack my skull.

My skull was jarred at least six millimeters from my spine. The ligaments attaching the base of my skull to my spine snapped. The only reason I survived was because someone made sure my neck was supported.

I wasn't thinking of my good Samaritan at the time.

Instead, I was thinking about how long I was going to be laid up. Even after a "miracle surgery."

I also wanted to talk to my husband. After all, I was injured and stuck in enemy territory. He needed to know, poor man. The doctor promised me a Skype call, but only after I was stabilized.

"Lieutenant Irving?"

My eyes jerked towards the tall man who'd pulled up a chair beside my bed. He was dressed in plain clothes. He rolled up his white sleeves, revealing a tattoo on his wrist in swirling Arabic script.

Only my eyes could move at the time. My neck was pinned in place by a metallic nightmare of a frame. The surgery was supposed to attempt to reattach my skull to my spinal column.

I narrowed my eyes. "Don't know you," I whispered, my throat harsh and raw. "What's your rank?"

He chuckled, his dark eyes twinkling. "No rank. I'm just a civilian. I'm here to counsel you and prepare you for surgery."

"Then why the hell are you here in a war zone?"

"Because it's here I can do the most good. And I'm here for you."

"Well. Isn't that nice."

The man took my hands, and I would have given nearly anything to have felt his fingertips, whether it was for pain or for the pleasure of human contact. He turned over my hands, using his eyes and fingers to examine every fingernail and cuticle, every whorl of my fingertips, every bruise, cut, and burn. Then, he folded my hands across my chest. "Of course, your surgery is risky, Lieutenant…Anna, if I may? I heard that they will insert a titanium loop to reattach your skull to your spinal column. One of your ribs will keep the rod in place." He stared at my hands as he talked, almost matter-of-fact and as clinical as a doctor. "There is still a very high chance that you will never walk again."

My eyes blazed with rage and unshed tears. "Is this your idea of a pep talk?"

He lifted his head and smiled at me. His dark eyes sparked. "That depends. Are you feeling motivated? Enough to get up and walk?"

Dizziness swamped me. By the time I came back to my senses, the man was gone.

All that remained was the scent of something burning in the air.

****

We are the jinn. Perhaps man thinks he knows us. The genie in the lamp, the three wishes….

But such tales are not so simple.

We present man with gifts of visions and fortunes.

We can take on any physical shape we wish. Sometimes, we even fall in love…as I did with Anna Irving. I saw the beauty remaining in her broken and burned flesh. But that is not what made me love her.

It was something darker and deeper.

****

When I first arrived in Iraq as part of the U.S. troops surge in 2007, I was thrilled by a sense of purpose and duty to my country. I couldn't wait to explore like a child through the twisted streets and ancient buildings. All my life, I'd loved hearing stories about swirling sands, flashing curved swords, flying carpets, and mysterious people who worshipped a god differently than I did. I threw myself into studying Middle Eastern legends, which evolved into studying the volatile history and politics of the region.

After the explosion, my memory stopped working like it used to. I was like a jigsaw puzzle that fit together, but with the pieces all mixed up. The doctors told me I might never remember some things again.

But I did remember when I'd first arrived. It was a quiet evening, which heightened the tension of our escorts to a fever pitch. My heart thudded in time with the large wheels bumping along as the truck transported me and several new arrivals to base. As I peered through the dim windows, my eyes were drawn to a small mosque, tucked away like a little child in the blanket of darkness. I squinted, my nose and forehead mashed against the glass. Was that a ripple in the doorway? My pulse ratcheted higher in its rhythm; the ripple appeared to weave and pulsate like a heat wave.

Was I certain about what I had seen? I knew that I had to return to that mosque. And somehow, step inside.

****

I felt the mattress dip beside me. I flicked my eyeballs over to the man. My apparent counselor. A spark flared in his eyes, crackling like fire, then vanished.

I scowled at him, and he smiled at me, white teeth glistening in a darkened face. "Shall I tell your fortune today, Anna? I think it will pass the time. Perhaps what you learn about your future may be…cathartic?"

I grumbled something, my mouth twisting as I tried to talk. It was getting harder for me to speak, and when I did, it came out garbled and confused. "My…surgery?"

He smiled at me. "Let's talk." He leaned forward and whispered in my ear. His breath struck my face like a blazing sandstorm, but strangely smelled of spices, incense, and something musty and forgotten. I wanted to recoil, but the neck brace and frame hindered my movement. "So…I see you as a survivor, but not whole. I see a heart burning with rage, made impotent because of the inability to act. I see that same heart hurt, little by little, by one it trusted, one it loved. And yet, this heart knows this one is not worthy of it. I see thwarted purpose…at least for now. After all, it is the future. It can be changed."

He moved himself so he looked directly into my eyes. "What can we do about it?"

My brain throbbed. Not with pain, but with something else that I couldn't define at the time. His words made my thoughts decrease to sluggish movements. "…what…do?" I almost didn't recognize my slurred voice.

"Yes. You're a woman of action, of purpose." His face blurred with sympathy. His eyes flared and were the only things I could see in sharp contrast to the foggy darkness. "It must kill you to be confined to your bed like this. Not knowing if the surgery will give you what you want. Realizing that your purpose as a soldier is in jeopardy.

"So, if you had three wishes, what would you wish for, Anna? If I were the one to grant those wishes, what would you ask for?"

I rolled my eyes. "…your…name."

He bowed to me. "Majd. A simple wish to grant."

****

Darkness filled the hospital ward, the silence punctuated by the footsteps of soldiers on watch. First thing the next morning, I would be wheeled into the surgery that might improve or worsen my fate.

Majd. I remembered from my studies that the word meant *"glory"* in Arabic. His words haunted me. On the one hand, I didn't believe in stories about three wishes granted. No matter how much I wished otherwise, real life wasn't like that. Out of all the Middle Eastern legends I loved, the ones that fascinated me the most were about beings of great treachery: the *jinn*, beings of fire, meant to lead man down dark, twisted paths.

But I couldn't deny to myself that my rage, my bitterness, my loss of purpose spurred me to perhaps believe the impossible. After all, what could really happen? They were just stories, right?

OK. I wish to walk again. Even if I'm not a soldier anymore, I still want to walk and be free to pursue whatever purpose I choose.

I breathed in quietly through my nose, then out through my mouth.

In the dark silence, there was an echo of a voice dark with fire and age. Almost familiar....

...Granted.

****

When I opened my eyes, I was groggy and nauseated.

"Lieutenant Irving? Take it easy. Everything is all right. It's just the anesthesia."

I groan, my throat crackling. "What...happened...?"

"You came out of the surgery just fine, Lieutenant. We've managed to reconnect your skull to your spinal cord. It will be a painful recovery, but we have heard that people with your condition do regain mobility."

"That's...good...." Through my puffy lips, swollen

tongue, and dry throat, my words sounded like a muffled jumble.

The doctor bending over me frowned and shined a light in my eye. "Hmm…we are going to observe you a little longer. I don't like the way your pupils are reacting to the light…."

Later, I sat propped by a neck brace and pillows, the doctor at my side as I spoke to my husband through Skype. I didn't know what to expect from him as his pale, anxious face filled the screen. I never doubted Abe's love for me. He seemed supportive of my passion to serve in the Army and find some higher purpose in life. But he was never good at managing the "heavy stuff," as he liked to call it. The curves, tricks, and nasty surprises life liked to throw in our direction, from the late-night phone calls from loan officers, to the constant bickering caused by his debts and his laziness to pay them. He always expected me to clean up his messes. He was appreciative, oh yes, and there would be peace until the next mess slipped us up again.

And yet, I felt confident in his love….

He scrubbed his hand over his face, bags sagging under his eyes, staring at my shaved scalp, stitches, braces, and burns. "Oh, Lord," he groaned.

"Hey, Abe," I croaked.

"Have they…did they find who did this to you?"

"No." I squeezed my eyes shut so he wouldn't see the fire that blazed in them as I thought about the faceless terrorists who planted the IED. My mouth tightened in pain and rage. *Believe me, I will find out, and then not even their god will have pity on them…*

I heard him let out a shaky sigh. "So…when are you

coming home?"

The doctor cleared his throat and talked about how I could return to the States after my condition stabilized, and I started the infinite hours of physical therapy. He cautioned my husband about the possibility of my complete paralysis, my honorable medical discharge, and gave only a small fragment of hope that I could emerge from this intact. I opened my eyes to watch my husband's face melt, his eyes huge and dark. "Abe…it's OK…if debts couldn't destroy me…neither could…a stupid bomb." My face twisted into what I hoped was a reassuring smile.

"Don't," Abe whispered. "Don't joke about this, Anna. Jeez, I mean, how the hell am I supposed to manage this whole thing? How do I process this?"

"Mr. Irving," the doctor cut in, "I understand that this is going to be a time of great hardship for you, but you should be proud of your wife's determination."

Abe shook his head and wiped his hand over his mouth again. "I just wish she…I wish it had never happened." His voice caught with a tremble that didn't come from tears. "I wish she wasn't over there."

"Well…I am." My voice hitched along with his. "I am, Abe…I wanted to be here…can't grant…your wish… but…I'll…get…better…." It was getting harder for me to focus on the conversation. My vision blurred. I didn't see Abe's small gesture of farewell, or even notice that the doctor had wheeled the computer away from the bed, presumably to carry on with the conversation.

I clenched my fists, preparing myself for the pain that would come from physical therapy, but I craved it. My wish was to walk again, and I was going to walk again.

In the weeks that followed, time blurred from pain, rest, frustration, and some minor triumphs.

I screamed obscenities at the physical therapist who tried to force me to rest when I wanted to keep going, even when my legs were still too weak to obey my brain's commands.

I cried when the words tumbling from my mouth made no sense to anyone, including me.

I struggled with nightmares, with whispers of doubt and anger in my own head. Every time I woke up and faced a new day, I lashed out at everyone who stood in my way or tried to soothe me. I wanted the anger because it spurred me forward.

I rejoiced when I could crawl across the mat by myself.

Crawling meant walking couldn't be beyond my reach.

Then, nothing will stop me from doing what I want.

****

When the jinn seek to possess man, we do so for many reasons.

Mostly, it's because we want to. Besides, there are many cracks within man's hearts and souls. It's so easy to slip in, and then, think of the fun we can have together.

Warriors through the ages see the darkest natures of man on the battlefield, in the hospital, in the training grounds. They are bred to be so strong and admirable.

But at the end of the day, they have to take lives. For their service, they get so little in return.

Anna Irving's heart already was cracked, but I had

to admire how she fought to make her wish to walk come true.

And I was by her side every step of the way....

****

Minor triumphs: the tingle of pins and needles blossoming up my legs and over my back, prelude to feeling.

At last, I knew I was ready. My jaw tightened as I hoisted my weight against the bars meant to support me as I tested my left leg on the floor. Then, my right leg. I took a deep breath and glanced over at the physical therapist, who nodded encouragingly.

Majd was waiting at the other end of the supporting bars. Sparks flashed in his eyes.

I screwed up my face and let go of the support bars.

For a breathless moment, I realized I was standing on my own two feet.

With my hands hovering over the support bars and the physical therapist standing by, I took my first steps.

When I made it to the other side of the mat, the praise from everyone around me filled my heart and supported me more than anything else had up until that time. But that feeling quickly fell away as I sagged exhausted into Majd's arms. "That's my girl," he whispered. "A wish well earned."

Back in bed, I couldn't stop shaking with elation. I felt power surging through my legs, eager to jump, run, dance, and walk again. But I agreed with the doctors; I needed to rest.

My eyes fell on the pile of postcards, cards from my family and friends, and an official-looking white packet on the nightstand. Carefully, I reached for the packet, struggling a little with tearing it open. I refused to ask for help with something so simple as opening an envelope, not after I had just beaten the odds and walked after being internally decapitated.

When I read the papers, I wished I had lost my head in every sense. After supporting my passion for the military, Abe, my husband, realized that he couldn't do it anymore. I knew he didn't have the strength to support me while I was injured, but I didn't want to believe it.

It was the note tucked in with the divorce papers that cut me deeper than anything else.

"I'm sorry, Anna. I love you…but I won't take care of you."

"Abe," I whispered, crumpling the note in my fist, "I'm getting better. I promise. Please wait, I can show you…."

Majd approached my bed and picked up the divorce papers from the floor where they were spread out in white piles. "I see," he hummed under his breath. "How funny that the greatest moments in someone's life can be so intertwined with the worst."

My lips peeled back from my teeth in a snarl. "Shut up!" I hissed. "I don't need to hear meaningless crap. Just get me on Skype. Right. Now."

****

"Abe, what the hell?" I struggled to hold up the divorce papers which weighed a ton to my exhausted limbs.

Abe rubbed his face, his tell that he was anxious and

upset. "I wanted to tell you, Anna, but I couldn't...not while you were hurt...."

"I *am*...still hurt!" I glared at him, fighting the blurring vision. I couldn't afford to look weak now. "Se-seriously? Who's going to bail you out of...your...me-messes now?"

Abe's face twisted, but it might have been my vision that made his face appear more monstrous. "Well, look at the mess *you're* in, Anna! You shouldn't have been on the front lines at all!"

My tongue felt like it was swelling inside my mouth. My eyes and fingers began to twitch. "Was...off-duty...."

"Even worse! This whole thing was pointless! And now...how the hell are we going to afford your therapy and everything else I now have to take care of because you nearly got yourself killed! I don't want this stupid burden!"

He made it sound like I planned to get blown up. My body twitched more as my eyes blazed. "I...ge-get...me-me-medical benefits...mo-moron!"

His eyes widened, not just from anger, but from shock. I normally never insulted him with name-calling, and my body was pitching and twisting. I heard Majd disconnect the call with a terse word and jab the buzzer calling for the doctors.

Distorted shadows surrounded me as my body thrashed around on the bed.

I don't know what they used to sedate me, but I felt it lick an icy burn through my veins. I lay there, chest heaving, fighting the drowsiness, as the doctors walked away, the words "seizures," "possible brain injury," and "more surgery" echoing in my ears.

Majd drifted over to my bed from the shadows and

knelt down. His smile was sorrowful as he stroked my shaved head and then my cheek. "My beautiful Anna," he sighed. "Such misery inflicted upon you, yet you remain so strong."

He leaned closer to whisper in my ear. "You have one wish left. What will it be, Anna?"

A sound came from my lips that might have been "...not...real...."

"Are you certain? Your other wishes have been granted. You know my name and you can walk." Fire sparked in his eyes. "I would say that's quite real, wouldn't you?"

His finger moved over the curve of my chin. I flinched from his touch, the room pitching in my vision. "...kind of...counselor...are you?" I breathed.

My vision was full of shadows. I couldn't be sure, but I thought I saw Majd surrounded by a nimbus of rippling mirage, crackling with a fire that I couldn't see, but only feel. I gripped the sheets as fear burst through the fog, surging adrenaline through my body. But I couldn't make it obey me.

Majd's smile twisted into a smirk. "Why should you fear, Anna? It's not real, right? What's the harm in making one...last...wish?" He rose to his feet and stepped away from me. "But think carefully about what you want it to be, my love."

"Wait."

He paused at the door, looked at me over his shoulder.

I fought through the fog of the drugs to speak. "I...done...so much for my husband...for others...my country...I get...little in return....Now...my body...my mind...my heart...taken from me....

"Why...should I keep giving? When I...should be taking?"

Majd nodded at me from his position in the doorway. "I'm listening, Anna. Tell me your wish."

"I wish...for the power and strength to destroy the reasons for my pain."

A heartbeat of silence.

"Granted," he whispered. "If you're ready to pay the price."

****

The drugs took hold, and I felt myself fall through the layers of my heart and soul to that hollowness inside me. It was filling up with whispers of rage and vengeance. I let those vile voices drown the fragile feelings of peace and patience, and I opened myself to this hot power.

Other whispers joined the cacophony from within me. They pressed around me with the weight of anger, fear, sorrow, pain, desire, a host of emotions that could be easily corrupted.

I opened my eyes, fueled by a surge of power. I stood up and smiled as strength poured through my limbs. I felt heat crackle around my body as I walked from the ward and down the hall. I wanted to laugh as I passed guards and doctors, who were oblivious to my presence. I looked back and let a laugh escape my lips; I saw myself still lying on the bed, peacefully resting.

I left the hospital and base, reveling in being unseen. But I had a mission to fulfill, like a good soldier. *How will I find the men who planted the IED? I want to show them what happens when they mess with me.* I laughed, a hollow one that echoed as though from a tomb.

A voice rose from within me and around me. **Listen deeply. You will find their whispers in their hearts. We jinn always listen and shape the whispers that drive man to commit many deeds. Then, choose what they fear the most. Use that fear to strike at them.**

I listened to the whispers, humming around me, Arabic rolling into my ears, incomprehensible at first, but then I began to understand. At last, I honed in on two, their whispers were bloated with malicious glee from blowing up a female American soldier, an infidel.

An infidel, am I? Because I came here to free your people from sadistic madmen who like to spread hate? My lip curled a little, and a raw, scraping chuckle escaped. *What will scare you? How about me?*

I shook my head, feeling long rich locks grow from the black stubble that patterned my skull in reality. My legs strengthened as I stood straight and tall. Finally, I conjured swaths of silken veils and shawls to clothe my body in this form. I stepped towards the decrepit building where two men lived who were committed to terror. Two men who set the IED that exploded me on this path I chose to take.

They were too focused on a map of the area, dotted with places where American soldiers were known to frequent. There were pieces of motors, batteries, springs, and mechanical devices that could be put together to destroy so many others.

Stirred by the memory of a ripple in the doorway of the small mosque, I appeared to them like a desert mirage. "Don't scream," I whispered, fiddling with the pieces, smiling at them. I beckoned with one finger as they stood there, chests heaving with fear, the smell of piss as they stained their pants. "You should test these," I told them in Arabic. "See if they work properly."

Trembling, they nodded and put the pieces together. I breathed encouragement into their ears. "It's always a good idea to make sure things work. Then, you will better serve Allah." I gave them the controller so they could ignite the switch.

With a grin, I snapped my head back, showing the full extent of my decapitation. The bumpy ridge of my bones rose to the surface of my skin as my head sagged and dangled behind me.

"Boom," I whispered.

When the explosion shattered their house, I smiled as the fire and shrapnel swirled around me, and I was untouched.

****

Two down, one to go.

I flexed my hands and looked to the horizon. In this form, I knew no limitations of time and distance. I concentrated on my husband, and in a rush of flame and shadow, I appeared in front of our small townhouse. I heard the rhythm of his breathing as he rested comfortably in his bed. At peace, no responsibilities.

Rage coursed through me as I clenched my fists. I wanted him to really feel pain and loss. More, I wanted him to inflict it upon himself. I knew what would scare my husband. Me, broken and craving his assistance.

With a smirk, I arranged myself in our guest room bed down the hall from our bedroom. I left the door open and lights blazing. I opened my mouth to release a cry for help.

"HONEY! I NEED YOU!"

I almost laughed at the sound of Abe cursing in fright and galloping down the hall. When he entered the room, his hair mussed, pajama pants slung low over his hips, pale and wide-eyed, he saw me in the bed. My head was capped with black fuzz from being shaved. Angry red stitches covered my forehead, face, and most of my limbs.

The best part was the really high stiff collar meant to keep my neck stabilized after surgery.

I gave him an agonized pout. "Honey, I need to go to the bathroom. Help me."

Horror sent him stumbling against the wall outside the guest room. I sat up in the bed, removed the collar, and popped my head to the side, where it rested in gruesome sag over my shoulder. "Look, Abe. I'm so flexible now," I laughed.

He dropped to the floor and scrambled back like a crab. Fear poured off him in waves. I rose and staggered towards him. He screamed, slipping and falling several times in his attempt to get away from me. I kept walking behind him at a leisurely pace, a smile playing on my lips at the sight of his terror.

My grin widened as he crashed through the balcony window and hurled himself over the railing. I peered over the edge, then appeared beside him. I shrugged my head back into position as I gazed at his shattered form, glass puncturing and slashing every inch of his skin.

"I guess you couldn't handle the 'heavy stuff,' Abe."

****

Before I returned to my drugged body, I journeyed back across the ocean, and entered the small mosque. I leaned against the wall in the back, taking in the space. I closed my eyes, the sound of my breath in time with the bowing and murmuring of prayers. In that moment, I was where I most wanted to be and nobody could stop me.

Whatever the price I had to pay for my wishes, it was worth it.

When I sank into my sleeping body, I did so with a smile on my face.

****

This time, when I awoke from the anesthesia left over from this second surgery, I was calm and refreshed. I blinked my eyes at the doctor who explained to me that the seizure was a sign that my brain had been traumatized. He was going to find out more about it.

"Mmm…right…," I murmured, giving him a sleepy smile. "Want to see…Majd."

The doctor frowned at me. "I'm sorry, Lieutenant Irving. I don't know anyone by that name."

"Wait…what? He was my counselor. He was here…all along…"

But the doctor shook his head, and I lay back, puzzled.

A few days later, as I did my stretching exercises for physical therapy, I asked if the counselor Majd was around.

My physical therapist shook her head. "There is no one

here by that name, Lieutenant. Now, you got out of surgery a few days ago, so take it easy…"

****

Letter to Elizabeth Kenney, mother of Anna, from Samuel Nelson, Medical Chief in the US Army:

Dear Madam,

First, I must write to commend you regarding your daughter Anna. She was a fine soldier and an excellent comrade. She exhibited natural leadership and compassion constantly while on duty.

I am aware of your struggles with your daughter as she recovers from a devastating IED explosion. You wrote of your concerns about her undue aggression and seizures. Before she returned to the United States, we observed how she behaved differently, as well as being disoriented, confused, and aggressive. She complained of headaches, blurred vision, slow speech, and poor control over some of her movement. I understand that she is not the Anna you know. It is our opinion, through observation and surgical intervention, that Anna suffers from traumatic brain injury.

We are learning more of the symptoms and effects of traumatic brain injury, which several of our soldiers have suffered from during this war. As we learn more, we will be better able to offer support, therapy, counseling, and whatever our injured soldiers need to resume a normal life.

We are pleased with Anna's progress in physical therapy. She will likely never move as she used to, but we are impressed with her strength and determination. She keeps saying that this was a wish that was granted to her, so it will come true.

Please contact us at any time with any questions and concerns. We will be happy to help you, and we thank your daughter for her service.

****

We were shaped from fire. We can take physical form, and we are just as inclined towards good as evil. We are the jinn.

I sat in the desert sands, watching the sky streaked with sunset and bombs from man's war. The muted sounds of explosions echoed in my ears with a melody that's familiar and new at the same time.

I stretched, enjoying the sensation of flesh and muscles moving, and rose to my feet. A pity I have to surrender my fleshy form for a time.

I snapped my fingers and Anna Irving appeared by my side. I smiled at her confusion and outrage. "What am I doing here?" she demanded.

"Well, you've been drafted, if you prefer to think of it that way. Your wishes were granted, and you have a price to pay now."

She glared at me. I loved her grit and determination. It might not always be a good thing, but it's not for me to judge. It's for me to shape her according to the direction she chose. That was why taking the form of a counselor worked well for me this time, as it had many times before.

Her form rippled with the smokeless fire of my kind; her eyes kindled red in their dark depths. "What have you done to me?" she hissed.

"You did it to yourself, dear one. You wished for destruction, and now you can bring it upon others. All you need to do is listen to the whispers in man's heart and shape them towards destruction. It's so easy to do, and you will do the job so well."

She stared at me for a long time before sighing. "It was easy to do," she agreed. "So, no lamps that anyone has to rub? No imprisonment? I have limitless power, and none of the drawbacks?"

I smirked at her, offering my arm. She curled her arm with mine and rested her head upon my shoulder. "My dear, the real jinn are not entirely like the stories."

Inspiration

Whispers is an original fairy tale that began as a retelling of *The Legend of Sleepy Hollow* with the Headless Horseman. Some refer to this story as "America's fairy tale." However, the sheer act of writing morphed the story into something more primal. There are still super-subtle references to *The Legend of Sleepy Hollow*, if you know where to look for them. The final story takes on the mythology of the Middle East involving the *jinn*, beings who are beyond good and evil, and the popular motif of three wishes. However, be careful what you wish for…wishes will change you.

About the Author

Whitney Zahar hails from Virginia in the United States, and has lived in Taiwan for six years. She and her husband Chris are a team raising an active, multicultural son, while exploring Taipei's art scene. Whitney is a writer and editor for a local ESL publishing company, and is actively involved in Taipei's dramatic community as a performer, educator, librarian, and blogger. Her short story "Mama

Snake" appeared in TWG's *Peak Heat* anthology, and her travel writing has appeared in Go Overseas.com and Pink Pangea.com.

Li Man and the Fox Spirit

By Pat Woods

Our story begins at nighttime. The curtain rises on the grounds of a house. A cool breeze, a balmy antidote to the day's stifling heat, moves the leaves on the trees like a gangster muscling small-time hoods off his turf. Over a pond filled with delicate lotus petals and bloated koi carp, buzzing insects dance in erratic patterns. A peacock struts with arrogant self-importance across the lawn in front of the house, unaware that his only function is to add to the atmosphere.

A dilapidated house squats in the compound like a malignant toad, and from it emanates the pleasant thrumming of a zither played with more than ordinary skill. Here, perhaps, is the explanation for the house's shoddy maintenance; its principal resident is an artist, a musician, perhaps a poet, too wrapped up in his work to give thought to more mundane concerns. We forgive the state of his house, and pause to enjoy the irregular rhythm of the zither, unwilling to intrude upon this prodigy and his labours.

We are not alone, however. First, we notice a shadow pass across the soft red light thrown by the lanterns that hang from the gables. Then we see that the figure itself casts a faint luminescence, an ethereal glow all its own. Should we be surprised that the figure makes no noise as it moves, nor leaves footprints in the unswept dust?

No, not particularly.

Rather, let us follow in this phantom's footsteps—incorporeal as they may be—and transport ourselves into this artist's studio, there better to observe the following scene.

On a mat quilted with finest goose-down sits our artist, legs crossed, as you do, his fingers blurring over the zither strings like the midges outside over their pond. He is a young man, not particularly tall, his physique slender and untoned by horseback riding or martial exercise. Hair the colour of ink hangs down in untamed strands around a face possessing both spiritual beauty and a certain comely charm. His fingers and toes, for we can see his well-made feet protruding from a pair of tasteless silk pantaloons, are long and clever. Over a collarless tunic that once was white, and might be again if its wearer ever deigned to take it off and wash it, the artist wears a silk jacket that in no way at all matches his trousers. He is bent over his instrument, sensual lower lip held between his fine white teeth in a rather contrived expression of concentration; yet, summoned by an instinct that he cannot name, he pauses in his playing and looks up at the figure that now stands before him.

His hands stop, plucking out their last notes thanks to some kind of involuntary musician's momentum. He swallows.

The vision that stands before him is one of heartbreaking loveliness. She is tall, thin, and graceful, man's desire made flesh, with large dark eyes and ruby lips slightly parted. She wears a robe of almost translucent silk, by turns revealing and concealing just enough to frustrate. Her cheekbones could inspire Tang Dynasty poets. Though her ears are slightly pointed, her eyeteeth even more so, and her features perhaps a little too vulpine, a man would have to be remarkably perspicacious to notice such trivial details.

When she speaks, it is like music itself, albeit the sort that is usually accompanied by rose-scented candles and a strategic dimming of the lights.

"You are the poet, Li Man?"

"That is my name," Li Man responds, thanking the Jade Emperor that this is no case of mistaken identity.

"I am a wandering spirit, called by your divine playing," she says, sitting down across the zither from Li Man, close enough for him to feel the heat of her breath, which carries a hint of persimmon. "Truly, the gods must favour you to endow you with such talent."

"They are but unskilled pluckings, the best a poor mortal like myself can achieve," says Li Man. "If I could replicate even one note of your voice, I would smash my zither into fragments at once, knowing that I could never again achieve anything so perfect."

"Well now," the woman says. "It seems that your tongue is as skilled as your hands." She gives Li Man a look that makes his mouth as dry as a mule's back on a hot day.

"That's good to know."

With impeccable comic timing, Li Man's twitching fingers produce a *duaangng* noise from the zither, providing a cheap laugh for those who like that kind of thing.

"I humbly beg your pardon," he says, "but are you a fox spirit? If I am wrong and have insulted you, I'll happily cut off my foolish tongue with a kitchen knife."

"Save your tongue, Li Man," says the woman. "You're going to need it."

Duaangng! went the zither strings.

"If it is my music that's drawn you here," Li Man stutters, "then it would be my pleasure to play for you. If my skill proves insufficient, I'll gladly immerse my clumsy hands in boiling peanut oil."

"I don't want you to play for me," says the fox spirit, for plainly she is one. "I want you to play *with* me." With that she stands, and with a deft movement lets fall her robe. Underneath, her body has more curves than the road to Houshan.

Li Man, unable to help himself, also scrambles to his feet, his eagerness straining against his gaudy pantaloons.

"If you will grant this humble musician the privilege of making love to you," he babbles, "then I will be as tender and gentle as a butterfly. If I do not satisfy you, I'll be pleased to dismember—"

"Be quiet, Li Man," says the fox spirit, reaching out to take him by the hand and lead him to his couch. "I don't want gentle lovemaking. I want to screw your brains out."

Duaangng! went the zither strings, all by themselves.

We turn away in rosy-cheeked embarrassment for a while, though the noises give us a pretty good idea of what's afoot—and, more pertinently, abreast. The voyeuristic amongst us can get an appreciative eyeful by looking into a piece of polished glass on a side table. Our attention is drawn back by a high-pitched yelp, and we cannot help but cast a furtive glance over our shoulders. Li Man, the fortunate fellow, is being ridden rather forcefully, with the fox spirit raking her nails down his chest.

"Say my name!" she demands. "Say it, bitch!"

"I don't even know your name," Li Man protests, between breaths.

In her passion, the fox spirit does something foolish. "Call me Jiu Weiji!" she commands, drawing blood.

"Very well," says Li Man, in a very different tone of voice. "Jiu Weiji—I know your name, and with it I command and bind you."

Jiu Weiji freezes in mid-buck.

"Yes, you'd better get off," Li Man says calmly. "I don't fancy having all my *yang* sucked out. Lying dead in a cold puddle of sticky *jing*? I'd never live it down!"

Jiu Weiji is now displaying all of her fox aspect, crouching so low that she is almost on all fours. She backs into the corner of the room.

"Li Man," she hisses. "I know your name, and with it I command and bind you."

Li Man laughs, sitting up and pulling on his mismatched silks.

"What on Earth makes you think that Li Man is my *real* name?"

Jiu Weiji snarls and returns to her robe where it lies puddled next to the zither. "I don't know what you think you're doing. I was giving you everything you could have dreamed of, and more."

"I don't dream of dying, Foxy," says Li Man. "My dreams are a little more golden. I need your help to fleece Fang Er, the landowner in these parts."

"Pitiful mortal!" scoffs Jiu Weiji. "All this because you want to be rich."

"It's not for me," says Li Man. "Fang Er robs this province blind. He needs to get his just desserts, and I'll give the money back to the local peasants. They need it more than I do."

"And what is to be my part in this?" asks Jiu Weiji, becoming intrigued.

It's not often I meet a mortal like this, she thinks to herself. *This Li Man may be as cunning as a true fox, but he is still a man. He won't be able to resist my charms for long. I'll play along for now, just to see how good he really is. But the moment he lets his guard down, I'll get even, just see if I don't.*

"Take a seat, my nine-tailed beauty," says Li Man, and he takes wine and two bowls out of a scuffed lacquered cupboard and pours a drink for the two of them. "Let me tell you what I have in mind. I'm no great thinker, but I have some small skill, and I'm sure this scheme will work. If you don't approve of my plan, I'll gladly beat myself over the head with a *jin* of goose-feathers.

"Now, this Fang Er is a nasty piece of work. His father, Fang Quan, was a kindly old soul, and treated the peasants in his district well."

"What were they doing in the district well?" asks Jiu Weiji, confused.

"Old Fang raised his eldest son, Fang Yi, to follow in his footsteps and look after the commoners," Li Man goes on, ignoring her, "but rather neglected the education of his second son in that department. Fang Er was supposed to be a bureaucrat or something. But then the plague came through and carried off both Old Fang and Fang Yi, leaving Fang Er in charge. He's about as delicate as a rhinoceros in heat. He sends his men out to tax the peasants to within a pinch of starvation, while he sits at home composing bad poetry and eating twelve-course meals. He's had just enough schooling to think he's the next Li Bai or Du Fu, but I shit better poetry every morning than he can write in a month. Vain, greedy, and an all-round bad egg, he's a peach ripe for the plucking, and it's his vanity that's the key to pry open the lock." Li Man smiles despite his mixed metaphors. "And that, my foxy lady, is where you come in."

****

The next night finds us at a mansion which, while it bears some superficial resemblance to that belonging to Li Man, is in fact as different as a dragon is from a grass snake. One particular difference that should concern us now is that instead of the strumming of a zither, the sounds of two consenting adults thoroughly enjoying one another's company provides the soundtrack. Jiu Weiji knows her business, and is holding up her end of the deal with gusto.

And Li Man? He is not far away, the walls that surround Fang Er's gardens and the guards that patrol them meaning little to one with his larcenous skill. As is customary in such situations, he's puffing away on an unapologetically anachronistic cigarette, which he drops and crushes with his heel in a decisive manner.

Having satisfied himself that Jiu Weiji is on point, as it were, Li Man leaves to her it, gives us a conspiratorial wink, and melts away into the darkness like a dinosaur being dragged under by a tar pit.

****

It is the following morning, and Fang Er is in deep distress. However much he enjoyed the previous night's frolics, something just isn't right. The business of the mansion bores him. The administration of the province tires him. The ability to write even his famously low-grade poetry eludes him.

"I'm just not feeling myself," says Fang Er, carelessly wasting the opportunity for a dirty pun. "I'd better send for a doctor at once."

Before long, a wandering physician, who "just happens to be in the area," is found and summoned to the mansion, where, unbeknownst to Fang Er, he spent an hour or so the previous night skulking in the shrubbery.

"I'm called Old Wang," Li Man says, in feigned and feeble tones, hunching his shoulders and squinting with creditable false myopia. "People say I'm a healer, though in truth I am no more skilled than the next man. If my patients live, then I am lucky, nothing more, though perhaps they are luckier still. Nevertheless, if my poor council can assist you, great lord, then I will do my best. What are your symptoms?"

Fang Er details his complaint while the phoney physician nods sagely, his false beard waggling as if it had a mind of its own.

"This sounds rather bad," Li Man says, clicking his tongue like a plumber about to make bank. "I had better perform a physical examination, if your lordship will suffer my lowly hands to touch your divine person."

Li Man checks Fang Er over, poking, plucking, and probing most unnecessarily with hands that he has deliberately made icy cold by holding them in a stream before arriving at the mansion. Fang Er squeaks and fidgets throughout the whole embarrassing process.

"Dear me, dear me," says Li Man. "I've seen this kind of thing before. I don't suppose, Lord Fang, that you've recently had an encounter with a fox spirit?"

"What a genius you are!" exclaims Fang Er. "I was just about to volunteer that information myself. At first, I thought I'd had a wonderful dream, but now that I come to think on it, I'm sure a fox spirit visited me last night."

"You're a very fortunate fellow," says Li Man. "Most men who spend the night with a fox spirit don't survive to see the sunrise." He absently rubs at the claw marks under his clothes. "As it is, you've lost too much of your *yang*. In the south, they call this malady *koro*, and it's been the death of many a young man. Luckily, your abdomen isn't distended, or you'd be a goner."

"Oh doctor I'm in trouble!" cries Fang Er, seizing Li Man's sleeves.

"Well, goodness gracious me."

"What must I do? If you can suggest a cure, I'll shower you with gold!"

"I'm only a poor travelling scholar," says Li Man, with a timely grovel. "I'm not worthy to advise a great lord such as yourself. You must send to the capital and consult the court physicians."

"That will take too long!" wails Fang Er. "By the time one of them can get all the way to my province, I'll have wasted away. Please, Doctor Wang, you have to help me!"

"Well, what you really need is to replenish your *yang* humour," says Li Man. "You've had a cold *qi* invasion, so you need some heaty drugs to set you straight again."

"And do you have any of these heaty drugs?" Fan Er asks.

"Alas, I'm all out," confesses Li Man with many a crocodile tear, touching his forehead to the floor in front of Fang Er. "I can't afford to purchase such expensive items. I would happily pull out my own organs and make them into a restorative tonic for your lordship, but I'm old and frail, and they wouldn't do you much good."

"Summon my servants!" cries Fang Er, leaping up. "Tell them to scour the province for heaty drugs! Take them from old men if you have to—they don't need their youthful vigour anymore!

"Doctor Wang, o learned healer," he says then, turning to Li Man. "What can I do to repay you? Name your fee!"

"I couldn't possibly take your money," Li Man says, making with the excessive displays of oleaginous humility. "Just give me a simple meal of millet porridge and send me on my way."

But Fang Er will hear nothing of it, and though it is beneath his own dignity to dine with a commoner, he graciously allows Li Man to eat in his kitchens, and has his steward slip a string of cash into his satchel while Li Man isn't looking. Li Man, who most certainly is looking, helps himself to a hearty meal, and, looking on the cash as a downpayment, exits the stage.

****

Two days pass, and no heaty drugs are to be found, no matter how much money is offered, nor how many threats of violence are issued as motivation. Fang Er is growing desperate, quite literally feeling himself growing more weak and feeble by the hour. He can't rest for fear that he will not be able to rouse himself. His servants bring him hot ginger tea, ginger duck, and plates of beef and onions, but he knows that this won't be enough to restore his *yang*.

At last, one of Fang Er's servants comes across a wandering peddler clad in filthy sackcloth and smelling like a tannery on a hot summer's day. Going only by the name Hong, he is hawking his wares by the side of the road to Linhe. If we can hold our noses for long enough to get close to this rancid individual, we will recognise Li Man, a horsehair beard stuck to his face with foul-smelling glue, and donkey dung rubbed into his tattered rags. A pretty good disguise, by and large, though Li Man is eagerly anticipating a good soak and a scrub after this phase of the plan is complete.

"Tiger penis!" he calls in a voice made rough by cheap wine. "Bear's gall! Bull's balls! I've got them all! Panda tongue! Snake's ear! Lion's snout! Buy them here!"

As soon as Fang Er's servant hears this, he rushes over. Then, as Li Man's pungent perfume assails him, he reels back, beseeching the Supreme Emperor of Heaven for protection against evil. Pressing a scented kerchief to his nose, the servant approaches a second time.

"I'll buy the lot," he says.

"Be off!" growls Li Man, cursing amiably. "You're just a servant. You don't have the cash to buy a single curly hair off one of these ox testicles."

"My master, the eminent and respected Fang Er, will pay handsomely for your goods," said the servant. "Give me what you have, and I'll bring the money tomorrow."

"Fang Er be damned," says Li Man with a gleefully offensive gesture that blisters the air about his hand. "You must think I was born yesterday. You take me to this Fang, and I'll see that I get paid in person."

"Can't you at least take a bath first?" asks the servant.

"No I bloody well can't! You'd make a thousand fleas and lice homeless? They fight off the other parasites, while keeping each other in check so everything leaves me alone. It's a good arrangement, and I'll not go jeopardising it for any Fang Er. If he wants my stock, I'll come and sit outside his house and you can bring the money out first."

"It's a deal," says the servant, and together—or at least, with the servant keeping Li Man within shouting but not smelling distance—they go to Fang Er's mansion. There, Li Man plonks himself down in front of the heavy gates. The iron in them immediately starts to tarnish and the paint on their stout timbers peels and folds away like a retreating army. Fang Er's guards ready their bows, but the servant calls out to stop them.

"Let me in!" he cries. "This man may be lice-ridden, but he has the heaty drugs our master needs."

"Lice *and* fleas," corrects Li Man, spitting casually and scratching at himself. "Hurry it up, won't you? I don't have all day."

"You'll need to verify the quality of your goods, Hong," says the steward when he arrives atop the walls of Fang Er's compound, breathing through his sleeve as he too is almost banjaxed by Li Man's stench. "Give us a tiger penis or something."

"All right," says Li Man, "but you'd better play straight with me or I'll hang out here and drive all your visitors away. Here's a buffalo's winkle to get you started." He reaches into his filthy sack and pulls out the item in question.

"Toss it," shouts the steward. A few of the guards chuckle at the unintended double-entendre.

"How about I just throw it up?" says Li Man with a grin. "You still want it to have all its *jing*, right?" And he lobs the phallus over the wall to the steward.

Not long after, the steward returns and lowers several strings of cash on a fishing line. Li Man eagerly snatches up the money.

"This ought to do it," he says, and ties the sack containing the rest of his goods to the line. "Pleasure doing business with you."

"We thank you for your help," says the steward, gagging as he pulls up the sack and some of Li Man's noisome odour with it. "You won't be insulted if I say that I hope we never have need of your services or your presence again."

"Not at all." Li Man farts in the direction of the gate, stripping off the remainder of the paint. "I'll be off, then," he says, but as he walks away, adds to himself, "Best not bother repainting that gate, old chum. I'll be back before the new moon."

And so things play out as Li Man predicted—indeed, as he has orchestrated. The heaty drugs procured at great expense from "Hong" do indeed restore Fang Er's wilted *yang* within a day or two. Soon after, Jiu Weiji pays another extremely convivial visit and, as if by magic, Fang Er's *yang* is back at low ebb. Hong is sought for, and eventually, when all else seems lost, is found.

"Thank goodness you're here!" says the steward when, more by smell than anything else, he locates the putrescent peddler. "You must come at once!"

"Hold your horses," says Li Man, who just happens to be holding a horse's you-know-what. "I've only just restocked! Do you think it's easy obtaining all this stuff?"

"Where do you come by it all?" the steward asks.

"Best not enquire too closely," says Li Man. "Why do you think I smell so bad? Anyway, I suppose your boss wants it while it's fresh. Got the money?"

A few more strings of cash change hands, and a short while later, Fang Er is reprieved.

After the third visit by the insatiable Jiu Weiji, Fang Er decides that, in addition to a large dose of heaty drugs, he needs the service of a Taoist priest to rid himself of the beguiling and horny apparition. One is duly found, and though he calls himself Reclining Lotus and wears a crane-feather cloak and a plaited silk band around his head, we know pretty well by now where this is going. By this ruse Li Man makes off with yet more of Fang Er's ill-gotten fortune, ostensibly spent on elaborate and useless exorcism paraphernalia.

So let us pass over this and diverse other cons, and advance the plot, such as it is, by several moons. Fang Er has become as an old and feeble man, and only a long convalescence will restore him to even a pale shadow of his former self. Most of his gold has found its way back to those peasants from whom it was previously pilfered. Li Man, back in his disreputable silks, is sitting cross-legged, as you do, on the floor of his studio. The zither is gathering dust in a corner, dreaming of *duaangng*. In its place upon the floor is the remainder of the cash Li Man has swindled out of Fang Er. Li Man, abacus clicking merrily away, is tallying up the final count.

Jiu Weiji, looking as ravishing as ever, and with a definite smirk on her luscious lips, enters, returning from an errand.

"You know," says Li Man, flicking the last abacus bead with his nimble forefinger, "that old scrote Fang Er must have been spreading lies about how rich he was. We've taken this game about as far as it's going to go, but the peasants in this province are still barely keeping their heads above water."

"Is that because they're still in the district well?"

"I mean they're still poor."

"They're peasants," says Jiu Weiji with dismissive disgust. "If they weren't dirt-poor, they wouldn't be peasants. Enough is enough."

"It'll never be enough," says Li Man, in as serious a voice as he has used throughout this whole escapade. "I know I said I'd let you go, but I think I'm going to have to keep you on for a little longer. There are plenty of greedy lords to prey on."

"Oh no. I don't think so," says Jiu Weiji. She digs into

her silk purse, which she has artfully sewn from a sow's ear, and comes up with a scroll of fancy-looking parchment. It is covered in neat calligraphy and bears a heavy official seal. A dank purple mist swirls about it.

"While you've been busy counting cash, I went to see the lawyers over in the spirit world."

"I don't like the sound of this," remarks Li Man, shooting us a nervous look.

"The ghost lawyers are a dreadfully stiff-shirted bunch, but like all good *yamen*, dead or alive, they'll take a bribe as soon as look at you. It only took me half an hour to get what I needed."

"Jiu Weiji," says Li Man, hurriedly but hopelessly, "I know your name, and with it I command and bind you."

Jiu Weiji grins and flourishes the scroll. "You can keep calling me that, but it won't do you any good, you little runt. I've legally changed my name, and now you have no power over me."

"Ah, well," says Li Man, getting slowly to his feet and eyeing the exits. "No harm, no foul? Live and let live? *Pro bono publico*, and all that?"

"Oh no," says the fox spirit, reaching once more into her sow's ear purse. "Bygones are most certainly not bygones." This time she produces a lash of cruel and fearsome aspect, a nine-tailed flail that looks capable of shredding a man's flesh right off his bones.

"Now, hold on." Li Man raises his hands. "I've always heard that while fox spirits can kill a fellow in extremely pleasurable ways, you're not allowed to physically harm mortals, right?" Though he affects calm, Li Man is very concerned indeed.

"We'll see about that," smiles the fox, shaking out her lash.

"Surely we can come to some kind of arrangement? If it's *yang* you want, I've got plenty to go around—"

"Put a sock in it!" yells the fox spirit, advancing on Li Man.

"Wait!" cries Li Man. "You'll force me to do the one thing I'd hoped never to have to do again!"

"Beg for your life?"

"No, call for my wife!" Li Man cups his hands to his mouth and cries out "Hei Weimei! I know your name, and with it I command and bind you! Here I am—come and get me."

The fox spirit has stopped in her tracks. "You mean you're—"

"—already married? Yes, and to a fox spirit to boot," says Li Man apologetically. "Sorry, did I forget to mention that?"

The fox spirit makes ready to go for him with her lash, but already the wind is beginning to howl with cries of frustrated vengeance. The wooden panels that serve as the house's interior walls start to shake and rattle, and rolling looks a distinct possibility.

"She's been looking for me for a while," Li Man confesses. "I've gotten pretty good at hiding from the old battleaxe. She's got a temper that'd make Zhang Fei look like Confucius."

And lo, before the younger fox spirit can begin to chastise Li Man for his multi-duplicity, Hei Weimei arrives. She is older in appearance, though no less attractive for all that, iron-willed and majestic, an empress to the younger fox's concubine. This impression is reinforced when her red eyes fix on the being once known as Jiu Weiji.

"You!" she roars. "*Huli Jing!* What have you been doing with my husband?!"

And ever since that day, in that part of the world a mistress has always been called by that name whenever a cuckquean confronts her.

"Wait just a minute," says the younger fox, now on the defensive and backing away from Hei Weimei's incandescent fury. "First, he never told me he was married, and—"

"How dare you come between me and my husband!" cries Hei Weimei, and conjures into being her own nine-tailed flail, a brutal piece of work with metal chains and spiky bits. "I'll give you the beating of your life, you little trollop!"

This is all too much for the younger fox. She has been baulked and insulted once too often, and feels thoroughly taken advantage of.

"Bring it on, you old hag!" she snarls, and augments her lash with the iron poker from Li Man's fireplace.

The two immortal beings fly at each other, and things get all *wuxia* with the gravity-defying moves and appreciative noises from the audience.

In the midst of this epic yet criminally undescribed battle, Li Man gathers up his remaining strings of cash and a few personal items and slips away. The fox spirits are far too caught up in their steel-slinging dervish to pay him any mind, though when they find out, their howls of rage will split stone and tear deep furrows in the grounds of Li Man's house, which itself will not survive their contest.

Once out of harm's way, Li Man shows a clean pair of heels and legs it for several *li*. Finally feeling in the clear, he sinks down beside a stream, cooling his abused feet in the water.

"That was cutting it fine," he says to himself. "After I distribute the rest of this money, I'd better skip town and go to ground somewhere until those harridans give up the search. On reflection, it's probably best that mortals don't get caught up in the affairs of immortal beings."

Then Li Man laughs long and loud.

"Good thing I'm not a mortal," he concludes, and, veering into the fox form that neither of the female spirits suspect he possesses, vanishes into the gathering twilight.

Inspiration

This tale is twisted from the fox spirit stories found in Chinese culture, particularly Pu Songling's *Strange Tales from a Chinese Studio*. Female fox spirits are said to seduce poets, artists, and scholars, leeching away their energy in the process. These spirits are known as *Huli Jing* (狐狸精), which is also the colloquial name given to a man's mistress in Chinese culture, particularly if she is young, beautiful, and conniving. They are also known as *Jiuweihu* (九尾狐), literally "nine-tailed fox," as they are said to have nine tails. These creatures also appear in Japanese and Korean culture, where they are known respectively as *kisune* and *kumiho*.

About the Author

Pat Woods hails from Nottingham, England, and came to Taiwan for an adventure that turned into a lifetime commitment. He lives with his wife Zi, writes for a local ESL publishing company, is a performer in Taipei's comedy and amateur dramatics scene, and tries to find time to write fantasy and other fiction between all that. He is a member of Taipei Writer's Group, contributing stories to their published anthologies, as well to Five59 Publishing's anthologies and to Jersey Devil press. His occasional blogs appear at taipeiwritersgroup.wordpress.com

Glossary

Du Fu – Acclaimed Tang Dynasty poet

Heaty drugs – Traditional Chinese medicine that restores a person's *yang* (see below).

Jin – Traditional Chinese unit of measurement for weight, approximately 500 grams.

Jing – Semen.

Koro – A cultural syndrome in which sufferers believe their genitals are retracting.

Li – Traditional Chinese unit of measurement for distance, the 'Chinese mile,' approximately 500 metres.

Li Bai – Acclaimed Tang Dynasty poet.

Qi – Life force or energy flow in Chinese medicine, which exists in natural patterns in the body.

Wuxia – Move/Fiction genre in Chinese culture, meaning "Martial Hero," and which concerns the adventures of martial artists in ancient China, for example: *Crouching Tiger, Hidden Dragon.*

Yamen – The office/station of local bureaucrat or mandarin in Imperial China.

Yang – The active male principle in nature, also referring to hot, dry, and sun aspects, which, if not in balance with a person's *yin*, or cold, moist, moon, and female aspects, can lead to health problems (see *yin* and *yang).*

Zhang Fei – Historical figure from the Three Kingdoms period, romanticised in Luo Guanzhong's *The Romance of the Three Kingdoms* as a fearless warrior with a short fuse and a fondness for wine.

Matchstick Fallout

By L.L. Phelps

Originally published in *Plan 559 From Outer Space Mk. II*

It was always on Fridays that the school groups visited The Museum of the World Before. Tiffany was sitting in her office, sorting through the last of her late husband's paperwork, when she noticed the time.

Ten minutes until the hover-bus would arrive.

And it would be prompt. Everything in New Seattle was prompt.

Straightening her white dress, she stood and walked to the full-length mirror on the wall behind her desk. She frowned at the perfection she saw, a lie created by her imagery system. The visual implants worn by all in New Seattle projected directly into citizens' brains what was beautiful and good, clean and unmarred, and never what was hidden in the darkness of the underground city. Tiffany ran her fingers through her hair, which looked straight and soft in the mirror, but felt wavy and crisp to her touch. She then smoothed under her eyes, wiping at the tears she could feel, even if they were hidden from view.

"Don't you ever wonder what you really look like?" she heard Matt's voice echo in her memory.

"Do you ever wonder that?" she'd asked, amused at her husband's question. *"Do you think, perhaps, that I'm ugly? That if suddenly we were above ground and we could see in real light, you'd no longer love me?"*

She remembered Matt's strange look at this question, his head to one side, and she'd had the unsettling thought that there was some unpleasant expression on his face concealed by her imagery system. Yet she had set this thought aside, along with Matt's question about her actual appearance. That anything besides darkness was hidden from view was an idea their society was taught to set aside for the greater good.

In darkness, we find light. In light, we find life. And life is to be valued above all.

They were taught to be grateful for the images projected into their minds. Without their imagery system, they would live in darkness. Without the illusion of a pleasant world around them, their society would go mad and resort to the former evils that had led to wars, to genocides, and eventually to The Disaster itself.

It was Matt's refusal to accept this without question that had led to his being retired thirty years before his scheduled time. Matt could not respect others, the Elders had explained when they took him away. He instilled fear in those he spoke to. Tiffany had been briefed and interviewed and checked for any signs of Matt's so-called madness, but in the end, she had been allowed to continue on in society, even if it meant doing so without an adult companion.

"Ms. Tiffany, the children will be here in five minutes."

Tiffany glanced in the mirror at her personal daytime robot, Dot, who stood behind her, sleek white and silver, with wool gloves stretching from her hands to her upper arms to simulate human warmth, and a permanent smile meant to welcome requests for assistance. New Seattle's robots moved as fluidly as humans, but were always accompanied by the clink of metal as they walked. There were thousands of them throughout the city, outnumbering citizens three to one. They manually ran the air filtration system, the water and sewage system, and the various other operations that allowed the city's inhabitants to be healthy and safe. Tiffany, like all adults of New Seattle, always had at least one personal robot by her side to assist her in mediocre tasks, as well as to run the personal devices that allowed her to live a comfortable life. For nearly a decade, it had been Dot who came to her fresh each morning. The faithful robot had been essential since Matt's retirement in keeping Tiffany focused in her daily life.

"Thank you, Dot," Tiffany said. With one last swipe against her invisible tears, she moved towards the door. Dot opened it swiftly with one gloved hand while offering Tiffany her ID and keys with the other. They walked together into the long hallway that ran between the offices and main area of the museum. The expanse was projected into Tiffany's mind as a tubular roof of windows, through which could be seen the image of blue sky filled with soft white clouds, a dim yellow orb, and trees that changed to simulate seasons. That day, the trees were lush and green, a few with a sprinkling of white and pink blossoms. It was nearly summer in New Seattle.

"The students are first-years?" Tiffany asked.

"Yes," Dot replied. "And there is an abnormality in the numbers. Six boys and five girls."

Tiffany's eyebrows rose. "Uneven?"

"One of the girls in the class got sick," Dot explained. "She was unable to adapt to her imagery system, despite several attempts at installing a new one."

"So they retired her?"

"Yes. Apparently she was upsetting her companion, telling her of nightmares she had of things she claimed to see when her imagery system was broken."

Tiffany frowned at Dot, surprised by her candidness. "So the Elders are worried about this retired child's companion visiting the museum today."

"It is hoped the child's visit will go without incident, but you should be prepared to answer any questions she may have. The Elders believe you of all guides are best suited for such a potential challenge."

Tiffany smiled thinly. "Right. Thank you, Dot."

In the lobby, the class teacher and her seven robot aides had lined the children up with their childhood companions. The same-sex pairs stood hand-in-hand in the shadow of a dinosaur skeleton that extended from the ceiling nearly to the ground. The children's eyes were wide, their faces aglow with excitement for their first annual trip to the city's sole history museum. In her ten years of guiding school tours, Tiffany had never grown tired of watching the youngest of the students come in for their first visit. This time, however, she felt a prickle of anxiety, her eyes on the girl at the back of the line, a robot built to look roughly her own age holding her hand in place of a human companion. Tiffany wondered what it would be like to lose a companion so young.

Dot touched Tiffany's elbow lightly. "Shall we greet them, Ms. Tiffany?"

With a broad grin, Tiffany started down the polished marble staircase, her arms open wide. "Welcome, children, to The Museum of the World Before!"

Tiffany brought them first to the exhibit of prehistoric ocean creatures, which displayed the progression of early life on Earth in holograms. They glided down a pathway moved steadily along by the dozen museum-issued robots responsible for the comfort of the tour. The children watched the projections, amazed and giggling, as floating images of single-celled eukaryotes were replaced by multicellular organisms, then dinoflagellates, then eventually protozoa, and then, faster and faster, larger and more complex creatures, until at the end of the moving pathway, life crawled onto a sandy shore. Then, on they went to the second display, through holograms of beaches and jungles and plains, past animals that had moved on land in prehistory and those which were recorded in images and drawings. At the final hologram, where a pair of *Homo sapiens* stood smiling with their young, Tiffany delivered the words she had heard herself two and a half decades before.

"Life is precious, boys and girls. For you to be here now took billions of years, with a countless number of generations and ancestors, struggles and triumphs. We must live accordingly, valuing ourselves and each other and the

152

life that's been given to us."

All the children smiled and nodded except the companionless girl, who stood apart from her classmates, staring at the final hologram image, her head to one side. With a nudge from her robot-companion, she offered Tiffany a smile that seemed smudged, as if past the projected image there was a true, more raw emotion getting through. It reminded Tiffany so much of Matt that she swayed, only to be steadied by Dot's ready hand.

"**Life is to be valued above all**," the girl said in a small voice.

"Yes," Tiffany said, and moved the group onward.

Next was the exhibit deemed the most important, as it was the one that showed the horrors of war, of hatred and greed and prejudice and discrimination. It was a display that reeked of the dangers of not respecting human life, and what evils came into the world because of this human weakness. It was uncomfortable, this part, but something the children would see year after year, until it was ingrained in them as it had been each generation in New Seattle before them. It was the only bit of horror they saw in their lives, and it always had the same effect. The children's breathing would slow, and their hands would move, and twist, and fold. Tiffany felt certain they were crying beneath their projected masks, just as she herself had cried every time she had seen the same horrors when she was a child.

"We must never forget, children," Tiffany said at the end of the exhibit, turning her back to a hologram of a city devastated by bombs, "how easily we can slip into these horrors again."

Tiffany glanced at the companionless girl before

ushering the group forward, and saw her eyes lingering on an image of a starving child. When the girl noticed her attention, Tiffany thought she was going to speak, but with one look at her robot, she remained silent.

Following this was the hands-on display meant to calm the reaction to the previous exhibit. Tiffany liked this part the least, the physical objects that rotated being on display always rough and unpleasant in her hand as she held them out for the children to touch. As a child it had delighted her, as it did these children. Their giggles of excitement were almost contagious after touching each object and finding that for once, the ugliness they felt harmonized with the ugliness they were allowed to see. Tiffany described the use of the objects one by one: the rusted pocket watch, the water-damaged book, the broken toy train. And then came the box of matches.

She held up the box and withdrew a single match as she had countless times, and demonstrated the movement needed to produce the small flame on the match's tip. "The tiny bit of fire was then used to make a larger fire for warmth or for cooking," she explained.

"They made fire?" the companionless girl asked as she moved closer, seeming eager for a better view.

"They did in the time before," Tiffany said.

The girl's forehead creased. "And fire made light, right? Natural light. In the dark. In the above. In the time before?"

Tiffany looked down at the box in her palm uneasily. This was the first time in her decade of work that one of the students had made the connection between the small fire makers and light, or at least the first time one had cared enough to voice such an observation. Actual light and all ways to produce it, natural or electrical, were no longer available or even sought after, for light would allow them to see with their eyes, which would override their imagery system, something they were taught to fear.

"Without our implants we'd see the roof of our existence," one of the Elders had reminded New Seattle on a broadcast months before. *"And the instincts that called us from the ocean, the ones that long for open air and land and blue skies and the sun would drive us into the dark oblivion of madness."*

"What if that's just nonsense," had been Matt's response. *"How do we know they aren't hiding something by denying us actual light? Maybe we're not even underground."*

"Of course we're underground," Tiffany had replied. *"Why else would we still have the visual implants? If we were above ground, it would mean the sun was shining again. It would mean we could start to rebuild. That's a time we anticipate, not one that would be delayed."*

But Matt's question had haunted Tiffany ever since, even when she had convinced the Elders otherwise.

"Do they work?" the girl asked, pulling Tiffany from her memory.

"What?"

"The matches. Would they make real light?"

Tiffany snapped the matchbox shut. "Certainly not. These matches are just to remind us of the life before. The life that will one day be again."

Tiffany slid the box back into its display and locked it.

"They look like they would work."

Tiffany opened her mouth, trying to think of a way to further assure the girl, but the class teacher, seeing her hesitation, stepped forward and put a hand on the child's shoulder.

"The Elders," she said, in an authoritative voice, "would not allow the display of something that would endanger our society. What we see, perhaps, are not matches at all, but a box and sticks free of the components necessary for fire. We are allowed this image to get a glimpse of something that was once important to the survival of humanity, but only as a device we may one day need again when our great planet is ready for us to surface. Take note, children, and remember."

She looked at Tiffany, wanting her affirmation, which she gave with a nod and a smile.

"Now, children," the teacher said, with a clap of her hands. "What is the motto of our great society?"

"**In darkness, we find light,**" the children chanted in chorus. "**In light, we find life. And life is to be valued above all**."

"That's right. Ms. Tiffany, shall we continue?"

"Absolutely," Tiffany said with forced enthusiasm. "Come, children, on to our final exhibit. On to the 21st century: the century of The Disaster!"

She asked Dot to lead the way, and waited until humans and robots were all through the door before casting one final glance at the matches locked securely in their case.

****

Tiffany sat in her office at closing time, her eyes on her screen as Dot moved a lever to keep the computer running. The robot was low on energy, her movements slowing as a

156

result. Usually, Tiffany would lighten Dot's workload towards the end of the robot's shift to conserve her energy until the night-bot arrived, but that evening, she had intentionally kept Dot moving as much as possible.

"Dot," she said, closing her screen. "Why don't you go ahead and go. I'll see you tomorrow morning."

"I'll wait on Tory, ma'am, in case you need anything."

"I'm going to have a quick nap until she arrives with the bike carriage."

Dot stood stiffly. "If you need anything—"

"I'll make do. See you tomorrow, Dot."

"Yes, ma'am."

Tiffany listened from her desk to the metallic clinking of Dot moving down the hall. As soon as there was silence, she slid from her chair and poked her head outside the door. Seeing no one in the dimming light of the projected hallway image, she made her way towards the main area of the museum, her keys pressed against her side to avoid the attention of the other museum workers and their robots still on duty. It wasn't until she'd slipped into the main museum and shut the doors softly behind her that she could breathe easily again. She smoothed her dress and walked quickly to the hands-on display room.

She was afraid the matches would be gone when she arrived, that they would have been reported as a danger and removed. But when she entered the display room, they were in the same place they'd been when she'd started her assigned job nearly a decade before.

"Do they work?" she'd asked then.

The curator at the time, a middle-aged man two years from retirement, had shaken his head at her question. *"What difference would that make? To use them would bring madness. "*

Or some truth about what's hidden in the darkness, she knew Matt would say. She had not thought of her question to the curator about the matches in years, and she had certainly not thought of the matches as a source for answers.

"OK, Matt," she whispered, positioning one of the match tips on the box's black strip. "Let's settle this once and for all."

The match lit with a snap and a pop, and then came gentle warmth and a brightness that stung her eyes. She dropped the matchstick in surprise, and blinked at the image of the flame burned into her vision. She waited, letting her heart calm and the image clear before reaching for a second match.

This time she held it. This time she looked up.

All around her were no longer the beautiful oak walls of the museum with its polished display cases, but gray stone slabs and rough metal cases. And above and around, where the light didn't touch, was the darkness she had always been warned of. As the match burnt down and stung her fingertips, she dropped it, and slumped against a display case.

"You see, Matt," she whispered. "Only ugliness and darkness."

When she heard the clinking sound of an approaching robot, she didn't move. She knew who it was before she heard the voice.

"Ms. Tiffany?"

"I'm in here, Dot."

The robot trudged in slowly, her limbs stiff with what to a human would have been fatigue.

"I told you to leave," Tiffany said, straightening and brushing off her dress.

"My job is to keep you safe, Ms. Tiffany, even from yourself." Dot walked over, and looked down at the box of matches still clasped in Tiffany's hand. "What did you see?"

"How do you know I used them?"

"There are two burnt matches at your feet."

Tiffany looked down at the polished floor, but saw nothing.

"Robots don't have visual implants," Dot explained. "We see the world as it is, but through night vision."

"What's that?"

"It doesn't matter." She reached out a single gloved hand. "Please, Ms. Tiffany. Give me the matches. No one has to know about this."

Tiffany frowned at Dot's outstretched hand, noticing it was shaking.

"Now, Ms. Tiffany," Dot said, her voice sharp. "There will be trouble for us both if they discover what you've seen."

Tiffany shook her head, confused by Dot's words, by what seemed to be a human display of fear. But just as she was about to question Dot, she thought of something that made the hair on her arms stand on end: Matt's robots had been retired when he was.

Dot was afraid.

"I haven't seen anything," Tiffany said, drawing a third match from the box. "Not yet."

She did it before Dot could stop her. The match lit with a pop, and a small flame grew between them.

And Tiffany saw Dot as she was for the first time. Not

metal and gloves, but flesh and blood. Her pale skin covered in dirt, her hair matted in clumps, her eyes concealed beneath black, thick-lensed goggles. And on her ankles were chains, the source of the clinking metallic sound that always followed her. It was the sound that followed the thousands of robots that worked around the city night and day, making it possible for humanity to continue its existence. Making it possible for the fortunate few to live in comfort while the masses slaved away in the darkness in which they were kept.

Inspiration

Having spent the past several years researching human horrors, in particular human trafficking, I am often troubled by how easy it is to live my comfortable life despite knowing human injustice is occurring all around the world. This story came to me when I saw an image on social media of a Third World child holding an empty bowl, next to a First World child holding an electronic tablet. I felt a little sick at the image, as it reminded me that so much of what I use and do is made possible because others are working, sometimes unpaid, sometimes as children, to make my life more shiny and convenient, and that despite all my cries for justice in the world, I too often accept what I see in the world around me, pushing from my mind what is hidden in the darkness. From this was born *Matchstick Fallout*, a futuristic reimagining of *The Little Match Girl*.

About the Author

Originally from the United States, L.L.Phelps is a writer who has made her home overseas for nearly a decade. The first several books in her fantasy series, *The Delron Chronicles*, are scheduled to be released beginning Fall of 2016. She is also at work on a crime thriller under her pseudonym, Ellyna Ford Phelps. You can follow her on Facebook as L.L. Phelps, or on Twitter at @LLPhelps1.

Buenas Noches

By Emily Brooks

Pedro leant against the bar, scouring the crowds for tourists. With their fair complexions, drab clothing, and stiff dancing, they might have well been wearing signs. Unaware, they sipped on overpriced cocktails. The upscale nightclub in central Bogota was a far cry from the slums where Pedro shared a single room with his older brother Javier. Its fake chandeliers and red velvet curtains shamelessly aspired to a dated conception of opulence, while DJs pumped out techno tracks that were popular with Bogota's young and wealthy. Next to Pedro, Javier rolled a cigarette as their friend Lucas swigged a beer. Dressed in white shirts and leather shoes, they almost looked as though they fitted in.

Growing up, Javier used to bring money home for their mother, a single parent. Both Pedro and his mother knew that the money was coming from crime, but there was an unspoken agreement. Their mother asked no questions as to how Javier got the money, and he kept Pedro out of it.

But after their mother's death a few years back, with no other family about, Pedro soon found himself getting a fast-track education on Bogota's criminal underworld.

Javier elbowed Pedro in the side, and raised his voice over the music. "So, if it were up to you, who'd you pick?"

Pedro's eyes fixed on a middle-aged man in a white shirt, sipping a whisky, alone at the bar. He leant towards Javier and pointed at his choice.

"Him. He's older, likely a business traveller. Probably has a fair bit of cash."

Lucas lit up his cigarette, took a drag, and glanced at Javier. "He learns fast."

Lucas's eyes drifted to the other side of the room and fixed on two young foreign women who'd just walked in the nightclub. One was a brunette, youthfully plump, despite her petite stature. Her curly brown hair draped onto her loose fitting linen shirt. The other was a tall blonde, wearing a tight fitting tank top and minuscule denim shorts that showed off her slender figure.

Lucas's eyes followed the blonde as she walked past them. "How about them?" he asked, looking at Javier with a smirk.

Javier scrunched up his face. "Nah, they can't be older than twenty. Bet they're still in college. They won't have shit."

"But did you see the tall girl's watch? Looked like a Rolex. Bet their rich daddies pump them full of money."

"But look at how they're dressed," Javier reasoned.

Lucas flicked his ash on the floor. "Foreigners always dress in scruffy clothes. Tell you what, you go talk to them. Bet you I'm right."

Javier laughed. "They'll probably just get freaked out and walk away."

"Then send Pedro. They ain't going to be scared of a sixteen-year-old kid."

Javier shrugged. "Sure."

"There we go Pedro, it's your lucky day," Lucas said, slapping him on the back.

Although Pedro's daily push-up routine ensured that he was well-built, his wide eyes and round face betrayed his age. Despite this, whenever Pedro tried to speak to foreign girls, they'd look at him in disgust, as though he was vermin that needed to be avoided. He turned back to Javier and Lucas, his eyebrows raised. "I can't talk to them. I wouldn't know what to say."

"Just buy them a drink and ask them where they're from," Lucas said, pushing him forward. "Well, go on. Don't just stand there."

Pedro swallowed, placed his hands into his pockets and made his way to the other side of the bar. He slinked in by the brunette and ordered a beer. Oblivious to his presence, she continued to talk to her friend as she curled her hair around her fingers. Unable to resist, he ran his eyes over her plump cheeks and full lips. The blonde spotted him looking at her friend and flashed him that familiar scowl. The brunette turned around. He waited to receive the same expression, but her deep brown eyes were soft and her lips curved into a smile.

Pedro jolted and his face burned crimson. "Hi, uh, I was just getting a drink. Uh, no, I mean do you want a drink?"

The blonde rolled her eyes, but the brunette's smile broadened as she raised the beer in her hand. "I'm good for now, but thanks for the offer." As he took a step back to leave, the brunette extended her hand. "I'm Sarah, by the way, and this is Jemma,"

Pedro wiped his clammy hand on the back pocket of his jeans before shaking hers. "Pedro. It's great to meet you. I don't meet many Americans. You are from America, no?" he said, talking rapidly.

Jemma put down her glass. "A good guess, considering you don't meet many Americans."

Pedro looked to the side. "I watch a lot American movies. So, what do you girls do?"

"I'm a student, but Sarah has a good job."

Sarah glanced at Jemma. "Sometimes I wish that I was studying too."

"Yeah, but then you'd be poor and in tons of debt like me," Jemma said.

Pedro narrowed his eyes at Sarah. "You don't like your job? What do you do?"

"I work for my father's company, an oil firm. Although it's a good job, I've always wanted to work in conservation. Complete opposite of what I do now," she said with a laugh. "But the company's really important to my father, and he wants me to carry it on." She paused to take a sip of her beer. "So what is it that you do? You look quite young, if you don't mind me saying. Are you still in school?"

Pedro shook his head. "I don't go to school anymore. I work with my older brother."

"What, like you're in business with him?" Jemma asked, frowning.

Pedro looked at his feet. "Yeah, it's a kind of business. A small one."

"Well, that doesn't sound so bad," Jemma said.

Pedro shrugged. "Sometimes I wish that I could do something else too, but, you know, we're family." He met Sarah's eyes and they exchanged smiles. "So is this your first time in Columbia?"

Sarah nodded. "It's both of our first times, but Jemma's been to Mexico and Guatemala before, while this is my first trip abroad."

Jemma nudged Sarah in the side. "You're such a badass, sneaking off while your dad's away."

Pedro looked at Sarah, who blushed. "My dad's in Saudi Arabia this month on a business trip. He doesn't know I'm here, and he'd be furious if he found out. He's a little overprotective."

"Shows he care about you. You're lucky," Pedro said.

Jemma snorted as she laughed. "You don't understand. Her dad has these weird superstitions. He used to be afraid she'd die if she went anywhere alone."

Sarah pressed her lips, her cheeks still red. "I have this aunt who's into sorcery, and when I was a baby, she fell out with my dad about his business practices. I'm not sure what he was doing exactly: all I know is that he was operating in a conflict zone. Anyway, when dad refused to stop what he was doing, she flew into a rage and cursed me. She told him that I would never become his successor because the devil's breath would poison me before adulthood, and I would never wake up."

Jemma giggled. "That story always makes me laugh. I mean, what on earth is devil's breath? Your aunt sounds nuts."

While Sarah and Jemma smiled, Pedro's face drained of

colour. "You don't think it'll happen, do you?" he asked.

"I don't, but I think my dad used to. Thing is, she once told my uncle that he'd suffocate before his fortieth birthday, and he died of an asthma attack when he was thirty-nine. But as I keep telling dad, I'm nineteen now and nothing's happened."

Pedro looked at Sarah, his face still pale, and forced a smile. "Some people have funny beliefs, no? My mom used to be terrified of black moths coming into the house. Thought it meant that my brother or I would die. Once one came in, and she wept all night. Nothing ever happened to us."

Sarah raised her beer. "Here's to our parents' weird ways of showing they care."

Pedro raised his beer and smiled at Sarah. "Well, I'll leave you to enjoy the rest of your evening. It was great meeting you both. Have a good trip."

Without waiting for a reply, he turned and briskly made his way back through the crowds. At the other side of the bar, his brother was standing alone. Pedro looked around, and then turned to Javier. "Where's Lucas?"

"Said he saw someone he knew and went to talk to them. So what did you find out?"

Pedro bit his lip. "They're both students, broke. Not worth our time."

"I knew it. Lucas is thinking with his cock again."

Javier glanced to the middle-aged man in the white shirt, who was still sipping a whisky alone at the bar, then back to Pedro. "Well, we can't be leaving empty-handed." Javier reached in his pocket. "Shit. Where's the stuff?"

"I don't have it," Pedro said.

Javier rubbed his forehead. "Lucas's got it. We'd better find him."

The brothers zigzagged their way through the mass on the dance floor. Strobe lights beamed onto the crowd of people. Javier and Pedro scanned the club for Lucas with no luck. They left the dance floor and circled the perimeter of the room, but he was nowhere to be seen. They went back to the bar, ordered another beer and monitored the crowds.

The evening wore on, but Lucas hadn't reappeared. Pedro had hoped to run into Sarah again, but he hadn't spotted her either. Javier finished his third beer of the night and slammed the bottle down on the bar. "That fucker's left with another chick again." He then reached in his pocket and pulled out his phone. His eyes narrowed as he read the message. He placed his phone back into his pocket, and turned to Pedro.

"He's picked someone up. Come on, let's go."

They walked around the dance floor towards the exit, passing Jemma, who sat alone at a table, sipping a drink. Pedro paused for a second as he saw her, before continuing to the exit. They stepped out onto wide boulevards framed by grand colonial buildings and skyscrapers. Javier walked just in front of Pedro with his hands in his pockets. A few streets over, they nipped into an alley between two blocks of office buildings. Parked next to a dumpster was Lucas's beat-up car. He sat at the wheel, smoking a rolled-up cigarette. In the back seat, a figure was slumped over. Pedro opened the back door and slipped inside the car next to the motionless body. He looked at the figure and his face turned white. It was Sarah. Her heavy eyelids drooped open and closed, revealing her pinprick pupils. Her head remained pressed against the glass, her limp body motionless, showing no reaction to their presence.

Lucas turned around to look at Pedro. "Good work, man. I was standing behind you, listening in for a bit. Bet she's loaded if her father owns an oil company. We might get a good pay-off from this one."

Javier glanced back at Pedro and scowled at him. Pedro looked down. Lucas turned on the radio at a low volume. Usually he'd blast the thing, but this was no time for drawing attention, especially as the cops often patrolled the downtown area. They drove out of the alley onto a wide, palm-lined street lit up by lights from towering skyscrapers. All the while, Pedro's eyes stayed with Sarah, watching her breathe heavily as he examined the contours of her youthful face. She looked so peaceful, so innocent.

The lights of the city faded as they left downtown. The grandeur of the colonial buildings diminished. Soon they came to the city's weathered houses that bordered the slum. This was where the holding houses were. That's what Javier called them anyway. Lucas, Javier, and Pedro would leave a handful of people at these houses every month. What happened to the victims at the holding houses wasn't their problem, or so Javier always said. Pedro knew well enough what happened, but he usually tried not to think about it.

The drug she had been given, scopolamine, was often referred to as devil's breath, and had some rather unusual properties. Its victims would fall into a semi-conscious delirium: becoming an empty vessel. They were suggestible, yet they remembered key details about themselves. Of particular interest to them, they remembered their PIN numbers. Sarah would be taken to an ATM, where she would be made to withdraw the maximum daily allowance. This would continue over the following days, as she was fed more of the drug, and her bank account was drained. When she awoke, she would remember nothing. If she awoke.

Darkness encroached as they entered the dense housing of the barely lit slum. They followed an unpaved road that cut into bare brick huts that climbed steeply up the mountain. Driving slowly along the narrow, unpaved roads, Lucas honked the horn to disperse the dog packs, which were rummaging through piles of trash.

They came to a shack with boarded-up windows and a thick metal door. Javier and Lucas got out of the car and dragged Sarah out. They propped her up on their shoulders and led her towards the shack. Pedro got out and followed them inside, watching her stumble like a child who'd just awoken from a deep slumber.

Lucas turned on the light, illuminating the naked walls and concrete floor. At the far side of the room, a staircase led to the basement. Javier and Lucas repositioned Sarah before taking her down the stairs that led to a dark room, where a singular bare lightbulb hung in the middle, exposing the mould that crept over the walls. Two dirty mattresses lay on the floor. One was unoccupied, but on the other a woman was sprawled out, with high-heeled shoes still on her feet and her pencil skirt ridden up. The light reflected from the huge diamond ring on her index finger. Lucas and Javier placed Sarah's flaccid body on the other mattress. Her drooping eyes looked through Pedro, and then rested to a close. While Lucas scrolled through messages on his phone, Pedro leant against the wall, his face grey.

After ten minutes or so, they heard the sound of voices upstairs, followed by footsteps on the stairs. Diego emerged, well-built, with a tattoo of a black snake across his neck. Behind him was Mateo, a lean but muscular man, with a huge scar down the left side of his face.

Diego lit up a joint and leant over Sarah's limp body. "So, what have you brought me today?"

"She looks half broke," Mateo said.

"Her father owns an oil firm. Found out thanks to Pedro here," Lucas said, slapping Pedro's shoulder. Pedro looked to the ground.

"Sometimes you can't tell just by looking. Mind you, that last one's turned out pretty well," Diego said. He pointed at the other women on the floor. "Maxed out one of her cards, but there's still cash on the other one. But we'll get rid of her tomorrow, so bring another one by."

Diego then reached into his pocket and pulled out a wad of cash and passed it to Lucas. "Thirty percent, as promised."

Lucas counted the money and slipped it in his pocket. "Thanks man. See you tomorrow."

Javier and Lucas high-fived Diego and Mateo and headed upstairs. Pedro's eyes lingered on Sarah a while longer then he trailed behind them.

Pedro, Javier, and Lucas lived on the other side of the slum, so they had to take the main road and go around it. As Lucas drove, he chatted with Javier about cash and women, while Pedro stared out of the window in silence. Lucas came to Javier and Pedro's small brick hut with its corrugated iron roof and stopped the car. Without saying a word, Pedro got out of the car and went into his hut.

In their single room, a few belongings were strewn about. Besides these, there were two single beds, a simple kitchen, and thanks to their criminal activities, a sofa and TV. Pedro went to his bed and lay down. Shortly after, Javier came in.

"What's up with you? You're being all quiet, and weird."

Pedro turned to look at him. "I'm tired, that's all."

Javier narrowed his eyes. "Alright bro, get some rest."

Javier went to the sink and filled a glass with water. He gulped it down, turned off the light and lay down. Within minutes, Javier was snoring lightly, while Pedro lay with his eyes wide open, thinking of Sarah, unconscious in the holding house. His bones chilled as he thought of her curse. Her aunt said she would be poisoned by the devil's breath, and never awake. It was too much of a coincidence. What if she died because of him? If he hadn't spoken to her, Lucas never would have drugged her. What if he had made her aunt's prophecy to come true?

****

The next night, Lucas pulled up, hip-hop blaring from the car. Pedro slumped into the back seat, his face solemn. Lucas glanced back at him. "Hey Pedro, what's up with you today?"

"He's been saying that he doesn't feel so good all day," Javier said.

"Some beer and a joint will sort that out," Lucas said. He passed back his joint, then started up the car. With the music still blaring, they left the slum, and headed to the other side of downtown.

They walked into a bar that was already heaving. Its expensive craft beers and trendy wooden furniture tended to attract an affluent crowd, which made for good pickings. The boys walked to the standing tables in the corner. While Javier and Lucas rolled cigarettes, Pedro hung his head into his hands.

"Hey, Javier, I really feel rough, think I'm gonna be sick," Pedro said.

Javier put his hand on his shoulder. "Alright bro, you go home. We'll be fine by ourselves. You want Lucas to drive you?"

Pedro shook his head. "Nah, it's not even eleven o'clock yet. I'll get the bus. Later."

He high-fived Lucas and Javier, then walked out onto the streets, where groups of people still sat on bar patios. He walked along the main road, away from the downtown area. A few blocks over, the houses became smaller, and the licks of paint less pristine. He saw a rusted bus approach and read the sign. It was his bus. He went to raise his hand, then bit his lip and put it back in his pocket. He stood by the road, watching the oncoming traffic. Bus after bus went by. Then he saw one that went to the opposite side of the slum. He reached out his arm and flagged it down. The weathered bus with peeling paint screeched to a stop. He jumped on board and passed a few coins to the driver. The bus continued along the main road that skirted around to the edge of the slum, which was barely visible in the cloak of night.

Pedro jumped off the bus and made his way into the

darkened streets. He passed though the brick shacks and heaps of trash, walking briskly as he ventured further into the maze. He recognised the shack that had a wooden platform jutting out from the second floor: he was getting close. He turned the corner, and the holding house came into view. Upon spotting the car parked outside, he tucked himself into a narrow alley. Lurking in the shadows, he watched the house, his eyes and ears sharp, like a predator waiting for its chance. The light inside was on, but no one emerged. He sucked in deep breaths as his barely blinking eyes watched the door.

Shortly later, the door handle turned. Mateo emerged, followed by Diego. Sarah hung over Diego's shoulder, her limp arms swaying like a dead octopus. He put one foot forward, then clenched his fists and stepped back. Despite being strong for his age, he'd never be able to take on Diego and Mateo alone. Besides, unlike them, he didn't carry a gun; his brother didn't allow it. He watched as Diego thrust her into the back of the car. The men got into the car and drove off.

The car returned less than an hour later. Still hidden in the alley, Pedro had not abandoned his post. They got out of the car, retrieved Sarah from the back seat, and dragged her inside. He breathed deeply, his eyes burning.

Shortly later they emerged, this time with the high-heeled woman. They were going to dispose of her. That usually meant dropping her off by the side of the road. The hairs on Pedro's neck stood up as they shoved her into the back seat, and left in the car once more. His body poised and ready, he listened to the engine getting quieter.

Under his breath, he whispered. "Not yet. Wait. Not yet.

Wait."

The sound of the car muted: it was time to strike. He darted from the alley into the house, turned on the light and ran down the stairs into the basement. He froze as he saw her: She lay in the foetal position, her face almost translucent. He snapped back into motion.

He ran over to her and shook her shoulders. "Sarah, Sarah."

No response. He shook her more vigorously.

"Sarah, Sarah."

Her eyes unpeeled then shut again. He picked up her shoulder bag and checked inside it. Her wallet and cards were still there. He flung it over his shoulder, then knelt down beside Sarah, and propped her up. He placed his arm under her legs and picked up her petite body, then carried her up the stairs. When he reached the top, he gently put down her legs and lifted her over his shoulder before leaving the holding house. He walked away, his pace quickening as he went. He ducked into one of the smaller side alleys. They might not be very long, and he couldn't risk being seen. His arms and back ached, but he could not stop: once they realised she was gone, they would no doubt look for her.

He heard voices in the distance. He stopped in his tracks, sweat wetting his brow. He repositioned her on his shoulder, and then continued at almost a jog. As he zigzagged through the alleys, his legs burned. The sound of the main road hummed faintly; he was close. Then, over the distant hum of traffic and dogs barking, a car engine approached. He stopped and stood by the wall. He was only one alley over from the small road they usually drove to the holding house on. He peered around the corner: the headlights approached. It was them. He watched the car pass, his heart pounding. As soon as he was sure that they were gone, he began to run. His chest burned and sweat dripped from his brow, but he would not stop.

The rushing stream of cars on the main road came into view. He continued running towards it, his thoughts racing. They had to get out of there, but how? He had a foreign girl flung over his shoulder who was drugged up to her eyeballs. When he reached the road, he placed her down on the ground and looked at her peaceful face. In that second, he saw who he was, what he was. This was his fault. He breathed deeply and waved out his arm to flag down a vehicle. Car after car sped past. Then, a black car stopped and rolled down the window. A man in his forties or fifties sat inside.

"Sir, please, you have to help me. My friend, she's really sick, you must help me," He pleaded, looking at the man in the car.

The man narrowed his eyes and looked at the girl on the floor. "She's a foreigner, no? What's she doing out here?"

"Sir, you must believe me, she's my friend. Please, we must go to the hospital."

The man pressed his lips, then nodded. "Get in."

Pedro placed her in the back seat and sat next to her as they sped to the nearest hospital. Sarah was crumpled up, still detached from reality. The man focused on the road, not asking any more questions, while Pedro watched Sarah's breathing become slower. The multi-story hospital came into view at the side of the main road. As the man pulled up next to the hospital, Pedro reached in his pocket and got out some cash.

"Here, take this, for your help."

The man shook his head. "No need."

Pedro tapped him on the shoulder. "Thank you, my friend."

He scooped Sarah into his arms, removed her from the car and ran towards the hospital. As he approached the front doors, the staff at the front desk spotted him and stood up. He glanced over his shoulder. The man in the black car was gone. He placed Sarah gently on the floor and ran his eyes over her face. A blue twinge stained her lips. Pain crushed his chest as he realised he was too late. With tears in his eyes, he leant over to kiss her. As their lips met, her eyes flashed open. He pulled away and looked into her eyes, his heart beating rapidly. She was safe now. He glanced up and saw two paramedics coming out of the hospital. He stroked her face, stood up, and fled.

He tore along the main road, not stopping to look back. Far from the hospital, he collapsed on the ground and gasped for air as his thoughts spiraled. He was a traitor to his brother, yet he couldn't stand what had happened to Sarah; what he'd done to all those people. He reached in his pocket and pulled out his money. It was enough for a long distance bus. He got to his feet and began to walk, knowing only one thing about his future at that moment: that he could not stay.

Inspiration

Buenos Notches is an adaptation of *Sleeping Beauty*, inspired by reports of tourists being abducted and robbed in Columbia after being drugged with scopolamine, more commonly known as devil's breath; a drug that is claimed to zombify its victims. Elements of the story were fleshed out during a recent trip to Latin America.

About the Author

Emily grew up in Wales and spent her early twenties in England before moving to Taiwan and marrying. Fascinated by the complex web of factors that shape our decisions, she draws upon her background working in mental health and psychological research in her writing. She is aiming to release her first novel, *An Insular World*, in early 2017, while working on her second. Her publications include an article on neurodevelopmental disorders for the UK-based charity Cerebra.

The King and His Three Sons

By Hugo Glin

As Prince Terrence, the third son of King Camaran of Stryermark, entered his father's chambers, the head of the secret police was finishing his daily briefing to his sovereign. "Among those pardoned as part of your Highness's birthday celebrations were Matty Gandy, Hank Thrower, and Ann Soochi, all members of the now defunct Non-Aggression Program, or NAP. Finally, there is the matter of punishment for households that flew neither the national nor the royal flag in celebration of your birthday."

The king, still dressed in his regal finery at the end of a long day of pomp and pageantry, poured himself a glass of schnapps and then slowly limped to his chair. Terrence knew that his father's gout was acting up again. The king turned to the crony and, with a wave of his free hand, declared, "Fine the lot of them. Ten gold pieces or the equivalent in livestock." Then he threw back the shot and placed the glass on the top of the liquor cabinet.

The young prince saw this as a typical demonstration of the king's decisive, forceful nature. However, he noticed that his father's head did not quiver like he always did after drinking schnapps. Also, the way the king purposefully set the glass down instead of hurling it into the fireplace, as was usually the case, added to the prince's apprehension as to this late-night summons of him along with his two older brothers.

King Camaran waved the police chief out and eased back in his chair. After some effort, he pushed his shoes off with his feet and gingerly placed them on the hassock in front of him. Exhausted by the effort, he closed his eyes and crossed his hands across his large, bloated midsection, letting out a low sigh. After a few seconds, realizing that his sons were waiting, he opened his eyes and beckoned them to sit by the fireplace.

Nigel, the oldest, sat closest to the hearth. He was the son of Queen Boleynear, Camaran's second queen after his first, Queen Kate, returned to her home country of Yberia when she had had enough of Camaran's flirtations. Nigel's chiseled jaw, raven hair and broad shoulders were the focus of fan clubs throughout the kingdom. He had grown into an ox of a man, taller and stronger than his two brothers and militarily more capable due to the wars he had waged in his father's name against numerous foreign enemies, as well as a the numerous rebellions he had suppressed within Stryermark. He was currently head of the Agency for Regulatory Rights and Essential Security Tactics, also known as ARREST.

Boris, the second son, sat in the middle. He was the offspring of Queen Ann Cleevige, the king's third wife, following Queen Boleynear's execution for adultery and out-flirting the king. Of the three brothers, he resembled Camaran the most, though his beer belly was not nearly as rotund as the king's. And no matter how often he patted down his thin, wispy blond hair, locks of it would rise at bizarre angles on different spots of his head as if static electricity was streaming through his body and out into the air. Boris was the burgomaster of the capital, which entailed issuing and controlling the myriad of royal warrants as rewards to palace cronies. Portions of the kickbacks received from the recipients that Boris did not keep for himself were used to fund various government projects, such as the one named after his mother shortly after her untimely death. The first act of the "Queen Anne Cleevige Program to Love Old Places," or better known by its acronym QAC-PLOP, was to replace the solid oak guardrails at the top of the castle tower, through which the queen had accidently fallen and plummeted to her death, which was the verdict reached by the hastily convened royal inquiry immediately following the tragedy.

Prince Terrence, the youngest, was dwarfed by the high-back chair he took. What Terrence lacked in size, brutality and greed, he made up for it with nearsightedness, for his mother, Queen Cathowl, Camaran's fourth wife, had taught her son to read in early childhood. Following the queen's death after accidentally falling off her horse and snapping her neck (as determined by another hastily convened royal inquiry immediately following the tragedy), the prince's disdain for the martial arts and the politics of the inner court took him along a solitary path of books and learning and eventually led to his appointment as head of the Department of the Research Catalogue (DORC) within the Government Efficiency Enforcement Commission(GEEC), a middling court position whose chief function was implementing the edicts and bylaws of the Sacred National Inspection of Publications, or SNIP. One of his duties was to control access to foreign publications. Fluent in a dozen languages, he personally read stacks of books every week. Over time, Terrence had amassed a huge library, half of which was illegal under the promulgation of SNIP's code, but, due to his position within the royal family, he was able to maintain.

Camaran leaned forward, resting his right elbow on the chair arm and placing his left fist on his hip. "So, I turned sixty today." He paused and then labored to swing his legs off the hassock and stand up. Once up, he scowled down at his boys and, in an ascending, accusatory tone shouted, "And you're probably wondering when I'm going to kick the bucket." His red-faced, scornful glare fell on Nigel and then Boris, neither of whom flinched. As the king turned to Terrence, who looked downward at the bearskin on the floor, Camaran's face softened. He knew that his bookworm son had neither the courage to take the crown nor the savvy to hold onto it. The king held out the five fingers of his right hand and said, "I've outlived five wives." He then turned the hand towards him, staring wide-eyed at the pinky, thinking of his fifth, Queen Ann Nakita Smyth, found accidentally drowned in the bathtub in the royal suite a month earlier, as determined by a third hastily convened royal inquiry. He quickly regained his train of thought and pressed on. "I have I have made the House of May stronger than ever. I have increased our lands tenfold, through diplomacy, with intimidation and even outright war." His voice mellowed. "For the first time in decades, we have peace." Again, he held out his hand and then said, "Five years of peace. Five out of forty on the throne." He sat down and slumped in the chair, the strain of ruling etching deeper into his face.

Nigel leaned on a chair arm and raised his left thumb to his chin and the forefinger across his mouth in a successful attempt to stifle a yawn. Boris also leaned to one side trying to part his buttocks. Terrence, however, simply stopped staring at the bear and was now looking at his father. Camaran bent forward and proclaimed, "I have come to the decision that you are to prove yourself worthy of the throne." He paused to allow the sentence to sink in. He saw Nigel lower his arm and puff up his chest. Boris simply raised his eyebrows as if he was waiting for a punchline. Terrence sat back in the chair, rested his elbows on the chair arms, folded his hands and placed his index fingers to his lips, returning his glance to the floor.

Camaran continued, "You are to go out and bring back something, anything, to prove to me that you will be able to ensure prosperity and peace for the Kingdom of Stryermark." He stood and finished with "You have a month to procure it." He then turned and waved his hand, saying, "Be off with you, now." He gingerly limped back to the liquor cabinet on his inflamed feet.

Nigel and Boris looked at each other and then both eyed Terrence, who had already risen and was heading for the door. The two older princes quickly rose and ran to the door as well. Once outside their father's quarters, Nigel asked Terrence, "So, what will you get Father?"

Terrence continued to walk down the hallway with his hands behind his back, deep in reflection. His answer was spoken in a low monotone. "At this point, I have no idea."

Nigel quickly retorted, "Bullshit! You're probably thinking about giving the old man some book from some liberal asshole, hoping he'll take it to heart and change things around here." He let out a guttural laugh and smacked his little brother on the back of his head, as he had done ever since Terrence was born. "You four-eyed dweeb. How's a book going to show greatness? I'm going to bring him a symbol of the grandeur and opulence of Stryermark and of the royal family, present company not included." He laughed again and then turned to Boris. "And what about you, Number Two? What are you going to bring back?"

Boris wore a pleasant all-knowing smile. "Oh, I think I know exactly what will get Dad's juices flowing." Then his expression changed to one of pondering. "The question is how to get it."

The next day, Terrence watched from his study as Nigel rode out with a dozen personal guards shortly after sunrise. An hour later, he saw Boris leave with two dozen city militiamen, as well as two wagons. By that time, Terrence had already changed from his princely garments to those of someone from the lower middle class. When Nigel had suggested a book the night before, Terrence was reminded of a story he had once read and he formed a plan. He would roam throughout his homeland to see for himself how its citizens lived. He would then return to the palace with this information to prove to his father that by understanding the people, a ruler could better serve them. He quietly slipped through a secret passage from his room and went to the rear of the palace. He had not left the grounds in years and he steeled himself for whatever he might meet as he opened the back door.

Terrence was first struck by the pandemonium of sound produced in the capital at mid-morning, utterly unlike the serenity found in the solitude of his library or office. As he walked, wagon wheels and pedestrians created a steady hum while hooves clopped a constant beat on cobblestones. Crates and bundles dragged across loading docks added to the din. Distinct voices of varying pitch and volume added to the cacophony. Next was the myriad of aromas, from the savory emanations of roasting chickens and pigs from restaurants to the gut-wrenching odor of open sewers; from the perfumed ladies promenading past him along a boulevard to the besotted tradesman stinking of cheap beer who stumbled out of a pub in a small alley and crashed into the prince. Even as the prince pushed the drunk off of himself, he reveled in the moment, a moment in which he felt more alive than ever before.

After getting up and dusting himself off, he turned a corner and passed an open door from which the whirring of dozens of spinning wheels emerged. Above the door was the royal seal, for the factory had received a royal warrant from Prince Boris. Terrence looked within and saw young girls manning each machine, hunched over and swaying with each push of the pedal. Some appeared to be no older than eight or nine.

"Oy. What business do you have around here?" The foreman, a large man with an imposing paunch, suddenly appeared in the doorway.

Trying to conceal his true identity, Terrence spoke with a foreign accent. "Oh, nozzing, sir. I have juzt never zeen zuch a zight."

The foreman strode up to the prince and looked at him from head to toe. "What the hell are you, some kind of immigrant?"

"I assure you, suh, I am not an immigrant." Terrence tried to soften the accent by changing the inflection, but this simply infuriated the foreman.

"Oy, you trying to call me a liar?" he shouted, attracting the attention of neighboring shop owners and their customers. As he pressed forward, he repeated, "What business do you have around here?"

"I was simply wondering why these young girls were not in school at this time of day," exclaimed Terrence.

The foreman walked right up to Terrence, who now realized that a crowd had grown behind him and prevented any escape. The foreman leaned towards the prince and shouted, "What are you, some kind of liberal foreigner trying to destroy our way of life?"

"Go back to where you came from," said a thin, bearded man approaching Terrence from the right.

"Yeah, we don't want any of your kind around here." From the uniform, Terrence determined that the man on the left was a stevedore.

"Look, I meant no harm. I was simply curious," replied Terrence. He had dropped the accent completely.

"Oh, so now you think you can speak proper, eh?" The foreman stepped forward and belly-bumped Terrence, who fell to the street. Immediately, the prince was bombarded with kicks and punches from every direction. He quickly went into the fetal position, protecting his head with his arms and hands. He had read about this technique in one of the books he had had to subsequently ban under SNIP guidelines because it taught the citizenry how to resist. He was about to start rolling around in an attempt to protect his kidneys, but he the sound of whistles slowed the beating and the crowd soon parted. Two constables approached and the older mustachioed one roared, "What in blazes is going on here?"

"This foreigner here was causing trouble." The foreman was pointing at the ground, even though Terrence had already pulled himself up and was standing.

The policeman turned to Terrence and demanded, "Let's see some papers."

Terrence said, "I can assure you that I am not a foreigner."

"Liar!" The crowd shouted in unison and then repeated the accusation.

"Shut up," yelled the officer. He turned to Terrence and said, "Show me some papers and solve this matter right here and now."

Terrence attempted to not let his face belie the dread he felt. "I have no papers," he said calmly.

"You see, he's a bloody foreigner," screeched a middle-aged woman.

"No papers, then you're coming with us to the constabulary." The policeman's large hand grabbed Terrence thin upper arm and he held it tightly. He nodded to his younger partner, who took hold of the prince's other arm.

Once again, Terrence insisted, "I assure you that I am not a foreigner." He pulled back on his arm with no effect.

"Resisting arrest, are we?" asked the leading constable. He looked at and nodded to his younger colleague again and they both struck Terrence on the head with their truncheons. Terrence fell unconscious to the cheers of the crowd.

Terrence was awakened with a bucketful of foul-smelling water. He found himself sitting on a stool with his hands shackled to a table. Both the stool and the table were secured to the floor. The stone walls of the cell were painted French beige. To his right, in the corner, stood a guard impassively looking down at him. The prince heard murmurs through the barred window of the thick wooden door, but was unable to determine what was being said. Suddenly, from behind him, he heard a wooden pail being dropped to the floor, but his chained hands made it impossible to turn around and see. As he strained to his left, he heard a whoosh and then felt a wooden rod strike across the middle of his back. He screamed in agony.

A gravelly voice spoke next to his ear. "So, you say you're not a foreigner." It pulled back from the side of Terrence's head and yelled, "Well, then you're going to have to prove that." Another whoosh and another painful crack, this time higher, across his shoulders. Again, Terrence screamed, but through gritted teeth.

Between panting breaths, the prisoner blurted, "I am Prince Terrence, son of King Camaran. I demand you release me."

Another whoosh and another crack along the lower back. "And I'm the reincarnation of Queen Ann." Whoosh!

Crack! "Prince Terrence? The same ass that recommended painting this interrogation room like this?" The guard looked around and asked, "Why the hell would anyone want this color?"

The other guard calmly said, "They say taupe is very soothing."

Whoosh! Crack! "Who gives a damn?" said the interrogator. He walked around in front of Terrence; he was a short man, barely five feet tall. He looked up at his colleague and complained loudly. "At least the old walls hid the blood and the mold. We didn't have to scrub down the place every week." He turned to Terrence, who was breathing hard through his teeth. "So you're Prince Terrence. Ha!" He flicked the cane and caught his prisoner on the left ear. "No one has actually seen that runt in years. They just use his name whenever they change something around here." He stepped to the side of the table and reached back with the rod. Whoosh! Crack. "For all we know, he's probably dead, like his old lady, Queen what-was-her-name?" He looked at the other guard, who simply shrugged his shoulders, barely altering his bored expression. The short man returned to his prisoner and shouted, "If you're a prince, then I'm the pope. Now shut up and answer me. Who are you and where the hell do you come from?" Whoosh! Crack!

The questioning lasted thirty minutes, by the end of which Terrence's shirt was ripped and bloody. The interrogator asked inane questions about Stryermark's geography and history in an effort to prove that his prisoner was indeed a foreigner. Through gritted teeth, Terrence answered every query and again insisted that he was royalty, which simply frustrated the inquisitor more. In response, he altered tactics and began dunking the prince's head in a trough. The whole time, the other guard remained in the corner, simply a spectator to the whole travesty of justice. By this time, Terrence realized that his princely claim had fallen on deaf ears and that survival was of prime importance. The sensation of drowning combined with the pain from his wounds caused him to pass out several times. In the end, the report insisted that Terrence was a spy and that further interrogation was needed.

Terrence was unshackled, dragged by two guards as he could not walk on his own, and then thrown into a tiny cell. He lay on the floor where he had landed for a few minutes, trying to gather the strength to stand up. The wounds on his back had not been treated and he felt them throbbing under his tattered garment. Eventually, he pushed himself up off the floor, stood and, for the first time, noticed his cellmate, a broad-shouldered, bearded man sitting in the dark corner of a cot. Terrence slowly, achingly sat on the edge of the opposite bed.

The cellmate spoke in a deep, slow, methodical tone, "So, welcome to the Hotel le Douleur. And what have you been charged with?"

Terrence lifted his head and allowed his eyes to adjust to the darkness in which the man sat. "I believe that should be 'la' Douleur, monsieur."

"Oui. I stand corrected." He moved out of the shadows and let his legs drop over the side of the bed. A long scab wiggled above his raised eyebrows. "So, we have a man of languages. Let me guess. You have been accused of being an intellectual."

"I understand that the allegation is espionage, though I have no recollection of being formally charged." Terrence could see a wry smile through the man's thick black beard.

"They tend to avoid formalities around here," said the stranger.

"What have you been accused of?" asked Terrence.

"Oh, the usual. Seditious acts against king and country, a distinct lack of patriotism, irreverence to the crown." He paused and then added, "Oh, and I published a book about basic human rights."

Terrence eyed his cellmate. "What sort of rights do you speak of?"

The man stood and limped to the cell door. "Oh, the usual. Freedom of speech, fair trials, freedom of religious belief, a parliament..." He turned to the small window and yelled, "...freedom from torture!"

"Oy, shut your trap before I go in there and flummox you." The shout echoed down the long hallway.

The prisoner responded by shouting, "The word's 'pummel.'" And then he quietly mumbled, "You cretin." He turned to Terrence, extended a hand and introduced himself. "The name is Paneer, Thomas Paneer."

Terrence shook Paneer's hand and tried to feign ignorance, but he recognized the name. Six months earlier, he had read a small pamphlet entitled *Common Sense* printed by Paneer's publishing house and had ordered it banned. His decision had been based solely on the guidelines of SNIP, as had all of his previous judgements. However, a copy of Paneer's pamphlet sat in his library next to other political volumes, the one section to which he often returned to reread. He now stood and faced his cellmate.

"Nice to meet you. My name is…." He paused as he tried to remember characters from a recently read play. "Sorry, I guess I got hit in the head too hard. The name is Hal. Hal Falstaff." He almost choked on the surname.

Paneer nodded and said, "Riiight." He let go of Terrence's hand, walked past him and climbed back on his bed. "Well, you best get some sleep. They usually like to get cracking at dawn."

Terrence stood for a moment trying to figure out what Paneer meant, but the physical strain of standing was proving too much and he laid himself face-down on the cot. As the growing darkness of exhaustion overcame the burning ember of pain, he again saw the faces of the girls in the sweatshop. His dreams became nightmares populated by the foreman, the street mob, the constables, and his torturer.

Terrence awoke to a wooden baton pounding on the cell door and the jangle of keys opening the lock. Slowly, with some difficulty, he sat up on the side of the bed and prepared himself as best he could for the coming abuse. As the door opened, two guards entered, went straight to Paneer's bed, dragged him out of it and then from the room. Paneer made no protest; he simply remained limp in the guards' arms. After they exited, his previous interrogator then entered, looked at Terrence and said, "Today is your lucky day. You are being released."

"And what of the espionage charges that were leveled against me?" He had totally given up on any accent, having realized that by this time it was as ridiculous as claiming to be a prince.

Whoosh! Crack! Terrence felt the bamboo rod across his

left shoulder. His knees buckled and he almost collapsed, but he recovered and stood up again. The jailer shouted, "What do you care? You are getting out of this hellhole. All I know is that I need this room and that means you're getting out. Now shut up and move it." Whoosh! Crack! "Move it, move it, move it!"

Outside the cell stood the other guard from the interrogation room with the same bored mien. He stepped up to Terrence, took his elbow and started ushering him to the exit. Halfway down the corridor, he said with slightly more enthusiasm than the previous day in the interrogation room, "You were only charged with suspicion of espionage. Well, we got ourselves a real spy now. They just captured Eddy Snowedin. We're gonna be real busy this week."

Five minutes later, Terrence found himself in bright sunlight outside the prison gates holding a bundle made from his coat and his shoes within. Standing in his torn bloody shirt and filthy pants, he let the sun shine on his upturned face, reviving him slowly with its heat and brightness. After a minute, he opened his eyes and saw small groups of people stopping and gawking at him. He feared that they might attack him as the mob had done the day before, so he quickly put on his shoes and coat and scurried in the direction of the palace.

Terrence bowed his head as he walked along the streets, grimacing as the thick coat rubbed on his beaten back. At the city fountain in the main square, he washed the blood off his face and swept his hair back with the water. He walked to the main boulevard that spurred off the square and led to the main gates of the royal residence, which he could see three hundred meters away. After being

193

unrecognized in the prison, he wondered how he would be able to reenter the palace without being thrown back into a cell. As he held his chin in his hand, he felt his swollen cheeks and suddenly turned to a storefront window. As he looked at his reflection, he first turned left, then right and finally nodded at himself with a small smirk.

He crossed the square and entered the main cathedral. He found a small niche along the left wall and entered it. After peeking around the corners to be sure that he was out of sight, he removed a shoe and then turned its heel. As he had hoped, the prison guards had not found the secret compartment where he had hidden five gold pieces. He pocketed them, exited the church, and walked around the corner to a haberdashery. While being measured, the prince insisted that the waist and chest be let out a few inches. He explained that he was going to attend a masquerade party that evening and was planning to arrive as a bloated noble. As the well-paying customer was always right, the tailor agreed to the wish.

While the garments were being made, Terrence first went to a bedding store, where he purchased a down-filled pillow and a white sheet. Next, he bought a few bottles of wine and finally he entered a wig shop. Using the pretense of a masquerade party again, he bought a wig made of short, blond, wispy hair. With two bundles under his arms and the wig in a coat pocket, he returned to the clothier to try on his new ensemble. Within the confines of the fitting room, he pulled at the strips of what had once been his shirt, reopening some of the wounds on his back. He bit his lower lip to prevent himself from screaming. He then wrapped the sheet around his torso, hoping that it would be enough to staunch the blood flow and leave the new clothes unmarked. For his plan to work, he could not raise any undue suspicion, which bloodstained clothing would.

He donned the new shirt and then thrust the pillow under it. After looking at his profile in the mirror, he then he put on the pants, carefully buttoning them around the bottom edge of the pillow. As he looked in the mirror once again, he saw that the clothing fit perfectly, including the waistcoat. As a final touch, he placed the wig atop his head. A proud, yet painful grin stretched across his face.

Before exiting the room, Terrence removed the wig and placed it in a coat pocket. He carefully wrapped his old clothes in the paper used for the bedding and picked up his wine. He paid for the outfit and walked out into the square in the direction of the palace. As he passed a restaurant, he noticed an alley that ran along the eatery's kitchen. He entered it and placed the old clothing bundle on one of the trashcans lined up against a wall. After adjusting the wig onto his head and placing a black floppy hat on it, he reentered the boulevard, his heart pounding with trepidation.

"Good day, Prince Boris." The proprietor of a tool shop bowed. "Would my liege care to inspect my wares?"

Terrence coughed and lowered his voice. "Perhaps some other day." Then he let out a laugh and said with a large grin, "Thank you just the same." He aped as best he could Boris's royal wave, raising his free hand quickly to the side of his head and ever so slightly twisting it at the wrist. As he passed others along the sidewalk, men bowed and women curtsied as they greeted the prince by saying, "Prince Boris, good day."

When Terrence had seen his swollen, puffy face in the window earlier, he saw a mask of his bloated, overweight, greedy brother, the burgomaster of the capital. Aping Boris was relatively easy, as his brother had a limited repertoire of motions he used when dealing with the citizenry: the wave, which was like an interrupted salute; the hearty laugh designed to make him seem like one of the guys; the cough to move things along when an event was becoming too boring.

As he approached the main gate, he had hoped that his performance along the road had been seen by the guards. He took heart when, twenty meters from the entrance, he noticed that the two sentries were no longer leaning on the wall, but were in fact standing at attention. At ten meters, an officer stepped out of the gate and greeted the returning prince.

"Prince Boris, back so soon?" asked the lieutenant after he bowed.

"Yes, yes," replied Terrence, trying to gain the courage to recite the story he had repeated in his head almost a dozen times as he had proceeded up the boulevard. "My men are camped out in the forest. I have returned because my damn horse threw a shoe and then threw me." He kept walking past the guards and was now within the gate. "The horse is being reshod as we speak and I wish to see the royal physician for this." He pulled back some of the fake hair to show his damaged ear. "I landed next to a briar patch when the damn horse threw me." After the officer had a quick look at the wound, Terrence let go of the hairpiece and opened the bundle containing the wine to show the man. "I bought this to help deaden the pain." He reached in, pulled out a bottle and thrust it at the lieutenant. "Here, share this with the men. A gift from an appreciative prince."

The officer took the bottle, quickly clicked his heels and bowed. "Thank you, your Highness." Terrence at once gave a "Boris" wave and then proceeded across the gardens that fronted the palace. Once within the residence, he went directly to his quarters. Since the princes were all gone, the servants seemed to have taken the day off as well, for he passed no one, much to his delight. When he entered his chambers, he collapsed on his bed. After a few minutes, he realized that he was still in disguise and quickly removed wig. He rolled onto his side, unbuttoned his pants and pulled the pillow out from under his shirt. Then he swayed back onto his stomach and fell asleep.

Thirty minutes later, Terrence was awoken by his servant, who had entered the room when he had seen the door ajar and was astonished to see his lord not reading, but face down on the bed. The prince instructed the man to fetch the doctor, which he did quickly out of fear for his liege's unknown condition. As the doctor entered, Terrence told the servant to lock the door. When the prince heard it click, he stood up, removed his tunic and shirt, unwound the bedsheet around his chest, and showed the lacerations and lesions across his back to the shocked men. Terrence then turned to the physician and threatened to hang him and his family if he told anyone of his condition. Terrence then instructed his servant to continue with the charade that the prince, like his brothers, was out trying to fulfill his father's wish. The servant was to use secret passageways to bring food and any news he may hear. Terrence then fell back onto the bed and passed out.

Hours later, Terrence woke up and immediately felt the bandages on his back, bringing back the nightmare of the previous day. He painfully rose out of the bed, got dressed, and proceeded to his library, which was adjacent to his quarters. After a few minutes, he found Paneer's booklet. Standing in a ray of late afternoon sunlight streaming in through a window, he read it twice. He then left the library, passed through his bedroom, and entered his study. At his desk, he wrote an official edict of release for Paneer and had his servant deliver it to the prison. He then returned to the library and pored over the texts dealing with government and philosophy, making notes within and without. The only time he stopped was for sleep, meals, and changing bandages.

By the twenty-first day, the scars were still pink, but they had healed considerably. As the deadline approached, Terrence continued to scrutinize tomes on political science. On the twenty-eighth day, Nigel returned with all but three of his personal guard, who rode their mounts tightly around a single steed, upon which a box wrapped in cloth was strapped to its back. Three hours later, Boris, with an arm in a sling, had also returned, but with only four of the militia and one of his wagons, which they guarded wearily, but closely as they passed through the courtyard.

On the thirtieth day, the princes were summoned to the throne room to present their gifts. Nigel entered first, followed by a servant holding a large plain ebony box and then a small entourage. Next was Boris, who no longer had a sling. He was followed by a beautiful, yet sullen maiden in a long white dress. Her long raven hair matched the hue of

Nigel's box, while her plain dress clung to her young figure. Finally, Terrence entered alone with nothing in his hands.

The king rose and said, "So, my sons, what have you brought me?" To Terrence, the tone of his father's voice seemed more expectant than anxious.

Nigel boldly stepped forward and signaled his servant along. "Father, I climbed the peak of Mt. Arschloch to its fabled cave, the Grotto of Destiny, of my destiny, and this is what I found." He pointed to the box, which was opened to present the largest ruby anybody had ever seen. "I vanquished a beast, a monster of a beast, in order to obtain it. And now you can use it to display our country's grandeur and riches."

As Camaran nodded, Boris stepped forward. "Father, I have sailed across the seas to find you a bride, a most beautiful bride, to make the winter of your life sunnier." He took the young woman by the arm and brought her closer to the throne. "She is not only beautiful, but she can also read."

Terrence saw that the king did not even grin at the sight of this truly stunningly beautiful woman. When Camaran turned to his youngest son, the prince stepped up to the throne, removed a booklet from his pocket and said, "In the hope that these ideas will raise our country to new heights and future glory, I give you this, Father."

Nigel barked. "Ha! The dweeb actually did get him book. What a dork!"

Boris chortled and said, "Well, Father, my gift can read it for you if you would like."

Camaran took the pamphlet and read the cover. He choked on a laugh, coughed loudly for a few seconds to free up his airway, and shook his head. He then mumbled, "You have all failed me." He sat on his throne, put his head in his hand, and uttered more loudly, "You are nothing but imbeciles." Then he pointed at Nigel and shouted, "You! In obtaining this rock, you say you killed a monstrous beast. In fact, you killed a bear, a Stryermarkish black bear, the symbol of our country for a millennium. Do you know how many of these animals are left in our country?" The king rose from his throne and glared at his firstborn. "A dozen. Eleven now, thanks to your stupidity."

Nigel reeled backward two steps and looked bewildered at his father. The king continued, his face reddening as his voice rose. "You thought I wouldn't know. My spies arrived here two days before you did and told me that you were already drying the skin. You bring me a new symbol of our country's grandeur after you destroy one that is emblazoned on our coat of arms, upon our national flag, within the people's heart." He glared down at his firstborn. "Do you not see the scandal you have brought on by killing an endangered animal?" He looked beyond Nigel, who stood flummoxed and defeated, and ordered, "Guards, arrest Prince Nigel." Two of the court guards stepped forward, took Prince Nigel by his arms and led him out. His sobs could be heard fading down the hallway.

Camaran turned to Boris. "As for you, you idiot, kidnapping the daughter of King Barry and Queen Michelle, even if it was the third daughter, was not taken lightly in Merca. You've destroyed our special relationship." The king fell into his throne as another coughing fit took hold of him. Though he waved off servant proffering water and assistance, the coughing persisted for almost a minute during which time Boris complexion changed various shades. Finally, the king concluded with, "In fact, their troops are amassing on the border as we speak. So much for my five years of peace, you putz. Guards, take him away, too."

Boris dove at the king's feet and clutched the edge of his robe. "But Father, I did it for you, to make you happy." As he was dragged out screaming, the king turned to Prince Terrence. Camaran's face was pale and haggard as he sat slumped in his chair. He clutched the arms of his throne and stood up. He retrieved the gift Terrence had given and spoke, his voice slowly rose in volume. "So, you think that by dishmantling the monarchy…" The servants and guards all turned their heads as their monarch began slurring his speech. "…and creating a parliament, that by guaranteeing freedomsh like speesh and presh and movement…" Camaran's breathing was becoming irregular and labored. "… that by giving every man and even every woman…" He squeezed out a chortle between breaths. "… the vote, you will bring proshperity and peash to our land!" As his voice reached a crescendo, the king's face, crimson from anger and exertion, seemed to slide downward on the left side. The pamphlet fell from his now-non-functioning left hand, but he pointed accusingly at his son with the right. His eyes widened from both the pain in his head and the realization that his son, the librarian, was about to become the king.

And that's what happened. Prince Terrence immediately assumed the throne while his father lay prostrate on the floor. His first order was to send an emissary to Merca to ask King Barry and Queen Michelle for their daughter's hand in marriage, thus staving off a war and reestablishing that special relationship between the two countries. His next act was to declare the release of all political prisoners to commemorate King Camaran's funeral. Over the following months, he had his brothers put on trial, Nigel for the killing of a member of an endangered wildlife species and Boris for sedition, and made them serve at least five years of their sentences before pardoning them. With his siblings out of the way, King Terrence began to implement the reforms that led to the establishment of a constitutional monarchy based on the philosophy espoused in Paneer's book, which sat on a shelf in the king's library next to Machiavelli's *The Prince*.

Inspiration

It is a variant of the Three Sons and the King parable, in which a king gives his three sons a test to prove their worthiness to be the rightful heir to the throne. Usually the older sons, who scoff at the youngest one's abilities, fail the test through their own character flaws, while the youngest usually comes up with the right combination of smarts, courage, and fortitude, and becomes the crown prince.

About the Author

Hugo Glin escaped from New Jersey at 18 and has lived in Europe and Asia ever since, discovering that the East sometimes does meet the West, but usually at a bar or in bed. In addition to a blog about expat life, *Me Love Taiwan Long Time: A Not So Serious Blog About Formosa* (https://melovetaiwanlongtime.wordpress.com/), he's had pieces published in *Roadside Fiction*, *Pilcrow and Dagger*, *Clever Magazine*, *Saw Palm*, and *Funny in Five Hundred*.

If you enjoyed this collection, please leave an honest review on Amazon.com, Goodreads.com, or wherever books are discussed online. Thank you to all the wonderful fans that have made this book possible and who continue to read us and review us.

About the Taipei Writers Group

Established in 2010, the Taipei Writers Group is an organization of writers interested in furthering their craft, and passionate about the art of writing. Members create poetry, short stories, novels, screen plays, non-fiction, and blogs. The group meets in Taipei, but members now reside worldwide. The group includes authors from many nationalities and backgrounds. Some write as a hobby, others as a profession. Some have been traditionally published, others self-publish.

We are committed to the advancement of literature and the art of writing.

For the latest news, go to https://taipeiwritersgroup.wordpress.com/ or sign up for the group's mailing list at http://eepurl.com/bg3dHn. The group will not send spam or pass on your details

21737378R00114

Printed in Great Britain
by Amazon